Trail Mix

By

LJNewlin

Reader Advisory

This novel was written for the ages of 13 and above.

All Rights Reserved. Copyright © 2006 Linda Joyce Newlin

TXu1-329-280

ISBN 978-0-6151-4085-8

Produced in the United States of America

Dedication

To my Husband Doug, who lovingly supports my artistic quests. To my sons, Jeremy and Ryan who taught me the joys of motherhood. To my father Donald Gustafson, whose death provoked a deep need to express my heart felt emotions in writing, and in painting. I thank God that you all have been a very special part of my life.

A special thanks to Frank and Sandy Ellis whose help with the editing was a gift from god.

Contents

Introduction

Included in this book are four short stories, each unique in story themes. The first story "Saving the Land of Zafer" is a fantasy about a brother and sister who must travel to a mythical land to save the queen from an evil curse. The second story "Kova" is done in an "Outer Limits" style. Here the reader finds that a nothing is what it purports to be. The third story "Forever & Ever, Amen" came out of an exercise from Stephen King's book "On Writing". This is my rendition of a relationship that has gone horribly wrong or otherwise affectionally known as the psycho wife. The fourth, but not the least of the stories, "The Incident at Green Valley Lake," a story of three adolescents who encounter UFO's, aliens, and their own fears in the quiet little town they call home.

Saving the Land of Zafer

The Hoffmans had survived the war and now they were in the process of piecing their lives back together. Lynn Hoffman was relegated to working part time at a five and dime store since the factories had all but shut down after the war. Work was difficult to come by so Donald Hoffman had taken a job on his Uncle's farm. It paid only fifty dollars a month but it had its advantages. His Uncle Roger renovated the old chicken coup into a small two-bedroom house. There Donald, Lynn, and their two children lived rent-free. The house was fitted with all the modern amenities. It had one electrical outlet, running water (as long as you primed the outdoor pump first), an outhouse, and a wood- burning stove. The stove doubled for cooking as well as for heating, which was very important to stave off the cold Pennsylvania winters. Donald and Lynn fought a lot these days, mostly about money.

The year was 1953 and Starr was about to turn six. She was born nine months to the day after her father had returned to the States. With school letting out for the summer and her birthday just around the corner, as far as Starr was concerned, life could not be better. She and her older brother, Billy, age ten, were walking home from school. It was a warm, sunny day, and they had almost three months of summer vacation to look forward to, so the long walk from Cory did not seem so bad. As they turned down the dirt driveway towards the house, Billy ran out ahead of Starr.

"Race you to the water pump," he yelled.

"No fair, you have a head start," Starr squealed.

Billy stopped in his tracks with his hands placed on his hips.

"Okay, okay. I'll count to ten, but you had better start NOW. One… two… three…"

Starr ran as fast as her little legs would carry her. Then she heard her brother count down "seven, eight, nine, ten" as fast as he could. She tried as hard as she could to run even faster, but as usual, Billy won. He was pushing the water pump with diligence, soaking his head under the cool running water by the time Starr caught up.

"No fair, you cheated. I heard you counting fast and that's cheating."

Billy scooped up water in both his hands from the trough and splashed it down the front of Starr.

"Mama's goin' to kill you. This is my best dress. She's goin' to whoop you good."

"Baby! It's just water. It don't hurt nothin'. What do you think Mama cleans your clothes with, gasoline?"

"Why do you have to be so nasty all the time?"

"Why do you have to be such a tattletale? Huh?"

Starr headed towards the house pouting with Billy right beside her. He figured she would not say a word about the water because she hated being called a tattletale. They had almost reached the front steps when they could hear loud voices from inside.

"I just don't see why you think you needed to buy another dress, Lynn, when you have two perfectly good ones hanging in the wardrobe right now," Donald blared out.

"Donald, my love, I think if the people at the five and dime see me in the same dress, one more time, they will run out of there screaming. I think if I see me in that same old dress, I'd have to go throw up."

"But you have two dresses. Can't you wear that pretty blue one I bought you? Once in a while, just for a change?"

"Donald, that's my church dress, I'm not going to wear my church dress to work. Anyway, I bought it out of my tip change. When it went on sale for a dollar-fifty…I just couldn't pass it up. My God, the material would cost at least that much."

"You know, if we are ever going to be able to buy a house of our own, we have got to save every penny." Donald retorted.

Billy and Starr realized this argument was going to continue for some time. Billy grabbed Starr by the arm.

"Come on; let's go down to the pond. We can skip stones or something," Billy said.

"Okay, but promise me we'll come back before it gets dark. It's scary down there at night."

"Don't worry. I'll be there to protect you."

"That's what I worry about. You think it's funny to scare me."

"Cross my heart, promise, we'll come back before dark."

The thickets of grass had already grown tall, and more trees seemed to have sprouted up overnight. They wove their way through, trying to stay on the old path, which was now almost completely overgrown. Billy had picked up a stick and was swinging it in front of him, trying to knock down the spider webs before he inadvertently ran into one. They walked a long way in silence until Starr broke in with a question.

"Billy, why do Mommy and Daddy fight?"

"I don't know. They've always fought like that."

"Why's money so important?"

"Cuz it buys things."

"What kind of things?"

"Lot's of things."

"Like what?"

"Clothes, candy and stuff. I don't know. Why do you ask so many questions?"

"Just wondered, that's all."

"I'm only ten, how am I supposed to know these things. Ask me what frogs are good for. I can tell you that, but this other stuff…"

"Well, what are frogs good for?"

Billy turned around with a great big grin on his face.

"They're for tormentn' little sisters."

"That figures." Starr said exasperated.

The water on the pond was as smooth as glass. Billy and Starr searched out the water's edge for flat stones to skip across the pond. Billy threw his first stone; it skipped four times before it sank. Then Starr threw hers, it just sank.

"You throw like a girl." Billy said mockingly.

"I am a girl, silly. How else am I to throw it?"

"Throw it from the side, not over hand."

Starr took a stone and side winded it across the water. It skipped six times before it sank.

"There. Beat that!"

"Well, you never would have been able to do it that many times unless I told you how."

"Fine, I'm done with this game. I'm going down to the beaver's house."

"They call it a beaver dam, not a house." Billy corrected her.

"Fine, I'm going to the beaver's dam then." Starr snapped back in a most sarcastic tone.

Last year, a very large, old beaver came to their pond and built a magnificent dam. It was a beautiful structure to behold. Billy even gave up bringing his fishing pole down, so as not to disturb its construction. They would both come down near the edge of the woods with Uncle Roger's binoculars and take turns watching the master builder in action. It was a good lesson for Starr, in learning how to be quiet. They were disappointed the following spring, when no pups emerged from Mrs. B's home.

Starr wandered down to the far end of the pond, partly to get away from Billy, but mostly to ponder the unique design of Mrs. B's now vacant home. She lay on the bank with her elbows planted firmly in the dirt and her head resting in the palms of her hands. Starr just couldn't imagine why anyone, man or beast, would ever build a house with its entrance under water. Everyone tried to explain it to her but she just could not make sense of it. She stared at it, examining every carefully placed stick and packed down mud, wishing there was some way she could see what it looked like inside.

Billy was busy still trying to beat his little sister's stone skipping feat. Periodically, he would glance over at Starr, to make sure she was safe. Just like his mama had told him to do. She was lying on the bank's edge with a stick in her hand making ripples in the water and watching them expand out. Then a rustling noise caught her attention. She signaled Billy to come over to her.

"Billy, I think Mrs. B. is back."

Billy plopped himself down next to Starr on the ground.

"Where? I don't see nothin'. "

"Right there! Just across the way. Can't you see the grass moving?"

What they saw next was anything but a beaver. They were in absolute amazement at seeing a small figure of a young woman stepping out of the grass thicket. She was not quite twelve inches tall but the most beautiful creature they had ever seen. She had long exquisite red hair, which sparkled in the sunshine. She donned a white tunic style top with black leggings, which were tied at the ankles. At the waist there appeared to be a short sword attached to a belt.

"I bet she's a princess," Starr whispered.

"No way, she has to be a warrior or a hunter. Look at her sword."

"A warrior princess then."

Starr and Billy's eyes stayed fixed on the small creature as she walked down to the water's edge. Her small creature's eyes were fixed on them. Just then, Mrs. B. rose up out of the grass directly behind their warrior princess, her large yellow teeth in full view. Starr jumped up and screamed.

"No, no, no, Mrs. B. Don't hurt her."

Mrs. B. scurried down to the pond's edge and laid flat next to the young woman. She mounted the beaver as one would a horse, and they both entered the water moving directly towards them. Both Billy and Starr jumped back as the beaver and its passenger came up on their side of the pond. The warrior princess dismounted and quickly shielded herself from the unsought rain of water as the beaver shook off.

"This is the human girl I was telling you about, m'lady," the beaver said in a low, gruff voice.

Starr exclaimed, "You...you talked! You're a **Mr. B**!"

"Of course I talk. I listen too. M'lady, the boy here calls her Star. You're looking for a girl child named Star. Is that not correct, m'lady?"

M'lady signaled Starr to come closer. Starr lay back down on the ground, getting as close to her as she dared. Her eyes were wide with wonderment.

"You did a good job, Annald. Now we will see if she passes the test. Come a little closer young lady, so I do not have to yell."

Starr inched forward.

"My name is Celine. I am the second eldest daughter of Queen Annabetje, ruler of Zafer. I have been searching a very long time for the girl child named Star. Is your name Star?"

"Yes, my name is Starr, with two R's, and that's my brother Billy. Why are you looking for me?"

"I am here to give you a test. To determine if you are the one."

"I don't like tests. I never do very well on them. Why do I need to take a test?" Starr whined.

"It's really a very simple test. If I tell you why, will you take the test?" Celine said in a kind yet coaxing manner.

"Okay."

Billy also inched forward so he could hear what Celine was saying.

"A while back my older sister, D'nasia took up with bad company. His name, Kutrell, and he is in league with a sorcerer who goes by the name Nhavan, who practices dark magic. My sister believes she is in love with this... this power hungry, self absorbed piece of excrement, and begged mother for permission to marry. My mother would not give her permission, for she could see the evil in Kutrell. So, my sister conspired, with the help of Kutrell and Nhavan, to rid our kingdom of their Queen. D'nasia, my beloved sister, snuck a potion into my mother's drink and she fell into a deep sleep. The Queen has great powers, and Nhavan would not have been able to cast his spells without the sleeping potion. Even with mother in this deep sleep, he could not kill her, but he did manage to steal three elements of her essence. They were hope, contentment, and restoration. He placed each of these elements in a human child upon their birth. We have found hope and contentment but without restoration, I am afraid she will not awaken. The priests of Zafer believe if all three elements are not returned to her body soon, she may never awaken. I believe you have the third essence of restoration hidden in you. That is why I am here to give you the test."

"Why would your sister want to kill her own mother?" Billy asked.

"Power, position, and wealth. With the Queen out of the way, she and that vile creature Kutrell would rule over the entire kingdom, under the tutelage of his eminence, Nhavan. As my mother's strength leaves her, a horrible darkness is settling in. The days are becoming shorter and for the first time in the history of our land, we are afraid that the crops will not come in. Our people will starve, but the taxes will increase to satisfy my sister's greed for things. So, I beg of you young Starr with two R's to let me give you the test to see if my mother's essence is hidden inside you. May I?"

Starr was deep in thought about the test when a loud, shrill shriek sliced the air. They all turned their heads in the direction of the sound, high up in the eastern sky. A mature male Northern Goshawk was swooping down in their direction. Billy jumped to his feet and Starr hid behind him as the great bird approached. Billy stood his ground protecting his sister and Celine. The bird of prey swooped around them and landed on the ground next to Annald, who just rolled his eyes. Much to Billy and Starr's surprise, a younger male version of Celine jumped off the bird's back.

14

"Wait, wait, wait, you can't give the test without me. What if she is the one? You have to have the orb ready to store mother's essence." The young boy said as he pulled a satchel off his belt and then dropped it on the ground.

"Young Starr and Billy, this is my brave and adroit brother, Tege. And as for you, my brother, where have you been, off exploring again?" Celine said shaking her finger at him in a reprimanding manner.

"Just a little. We must find new land to live in, if we don't succeed…if mother doesn't…you know."

"Don't talk like that. We will succeed; we have to succeed. Now give me the powder so I can administer the test."

Tege removed a small satchel from around his neck and handed it over to his sister. Celine opened the pouch, and then signaled Starr closer.

"This is the test Starr, I need to place this powder on your tongue and you must swallow it. Don't worry. It tastes sweet. The other children found it quite delightful. Then when I tell you to, you need to blow on the orb, which Tege is holding."

"That doesn't seem like much of a test." Starr responded.

"I told you it was simple."

Starr stuck out her tongue as she would for her doctor and Celine poured out the contents of the pouch. She smacked her lips a few times then swallowed.

"Ummm… it is sweet, like rock candy."

Celine and Tege watched Starr's eyes with the same intensity Starr's cat watched a mouse before he pounced on his prey. A flicker of light jumped from her left to her right eye. Tege held up the clear orb to Starr's mouth. "Okay Starr, blow on the orb, NOW!"

Starr took a deep breath and blew on the orb. Nothing happened.

"Blow harder Starr, like you're blowing out the candles on your birthday cake." Billy said.

Starr blew so hard it knocked Celine and Tege over. They stood up, brushing the dust off their clothes.

"I was afraid of this. It's stuck," Celine said with exasperation in her voice.

"There has to be something we can do. We can't allow the Queen to die. Tell us what to do and we'll do it, right Starr?" Billy sounded so desperate that Starr thought he would cry. She had never seen him cry, not even when papa gave him a whooping. So if it was that important to Billy, of course she would be willing to do whatever Celine said.

"Right," Starr said emphatically.

Celine played with a small pouch that hung around her neck, one that looked just like her brother's.

"Well, there is one other way."

She emptied the pouch into the palm of her hand. There, rested three pebbles, two of them resembled diamonds and the third looked like a small skipping stone.

"You will each have to swallow one of these, so you can enter my world for a short time."

"What's the other one for?" Billy asked.

"That's the hard part. Starr will have to skip it across the water at least six times. If she succeeds, it will open a door to a secret tunnel that leads to the Queen's chambers.

"Most girls can't do it." Tege taunted.

"I can skip stones. Can't I Billy?" Starr looked up at Billy desperate for his confirmation. Then she looked at the tiny pebbles in Celine's hand.

"But that's so small, I don't know if I can..."

Celine stuck her own tongue out to indicate to the children to do the same.

"Once you take these, then the stone will fit nicely in your hand."

With in moments after they swallowed the pebbles, their heads began to spin. Then Starr noticed she was looking up at Celine and Celine placed the skipping stone in her hand.

"Quickly now, time is of the essence."

"How did you get so big?"

"Later little one, throw the stone."

Starr took the stone and side winded it across the top of the water, just as Billy had shown her. It skipped seven times. She watched the ripples of the water expand out in a hypnotizing fashion. Then they both found it difficult to see. There was a cold darkness all around them with a faint flicker of light in the distance.

"Come now, we must move quickly. Tege, go grab the torch and bring it back to light our way," Celine commanded.

Celine, Tege, Starr, and Billy wove their way through a musty, dark maze until they came to a section that was much lower than the rest. Tege placed the torch down on the ground and slid it away from them. It flickered and nearly went out. He crawled on his hands and knees a few feet, and then placed his finger to his lips, indicating to them they needed to be very quiet. He placed his ear to the wall to listen.

"Is she alone…?" Celine whispered.

Tege, with his ear still planted against the wall waved his hand at her to back off and be quiet. He listened for a few moments longer, then signaled them to join him. He pulled back a partition just enough to let the light from the outer room hit his eyes. His mother was resting on her bed with her hands folded over her abdomen. He could not tell whether she was dead or alive, but he could tell she was alone. Tege opened the partition far enough for them to squeeze through. They entered the Queen's chambers under a table, which held a lantern, water bowl, and water vase on top of it. Tege helped Starr enter the room and Billy followed, bumping his head on the underside of the table. Celine was the last to enter the room.

"I'll obtain the other two orbs," Celine said.

She reached up to the end of the bedpost at the foot of her mother's bed. She removed the round wood ball and laid it open like an egg cracked in two, which exposed the first orb.

"Hide in plain sight, I always say." She said with a smile.

Celine placed one orb above her mother's hands and one above her head. Tege held his clear, empty orb over the Queen's mouth.

"Alright Starr, come forward and breathe on the clear orb." Tege said with a sense of urgency in his voice.

Starr pulled herself up onto the bed and breathed on the orb. A faint cyan colored light flickered inside and then grew. Tege let go of his orb, and it floated above his mother's face. As the light grew in intensity the other two orbs floated up, one glowing a magenta color and the other with a brilliant yellow. Then all three joined and swirled around faster and faster, making a bright white light, which darted directly into the

Queen's chest. The Queen abruptly sat up, taking in air as though she had been holding her breath under water for a very long time. Her eyes opened to see her beloved children. Celine and Tege hugged their mother with tears of joy in their eyes.

This embrace was short lived for D'nasia, Kutrell, Nhavan, and two of their guards bolted through the door.

"Apprehend those traitors. Throw my loving brother and sister in the dungeon and take those snot nose little busy bodies to the pit. Let the rats have them for dinner," D'nasia roared.

"NO!" The Queen commanded. She held her hands outstretched with her head tilted back towards the heavens. Then she glared at the five of them charging at her, and they stood frozen in time. "Take the children back through the tunnels to their home. I will deal with my dear daughter and her conspirators. Quickly now, time runs short."

Celine, Tege and the children ran as fast as the maze of tunnels would allow. They ran until they were nearly out of breath. Then suddenly, it was dark again, pitch black dark.

***

When word spread that the Starr and Billy were missing, people from miles around came to help in the search. They had been combing the woods for almost six hours with torches, lanterns, and flashlights when someone yelled out down by the pond.

"Over here. I found them! Over here."

The throng of people gathered around two small bodies that were lying in a grass thicket. Donald and Lynn pushed their way through the crowd expecting the worst. Lynn fell to her knees and scooped Starr into her arms, her skin was cool to the touch, but she was alive. "Wake up, sweetie. Mommy and Daddy are here."

Donald knelt down and shook Billy's shoulder. "Come on, Billy. It's time to wake up."

He turned to the sheriff.

"What in the world happened here? Should we call the doctor?"

Billy wiped the sleep from his eyes. "I don't need no doctor." Billy said through a yawn.

Starr's eyes squinted, as she tried to focus on the people around her.

"Hi mommy, where's the warrior princess and her brother?"

Lynn wrapped her arms around her and held her tight. "Thank God, you're alright. What are you talking about child?"

Starr and Billy looked at all the people standing around with concerned looks on their faces and then at each other. They decided, without speaking that they best not say another word about their little adventure. No one would believe them anyway. It would just have to be their little secret.

"Starr must have been dreaming," Billy said.

Donald now changed his tone and sternly demanded, "Why didn't you come home when you were supposed to".

Billy decided the best thing to do was tell the truth, at least some of it. "We heard you two fighting about money again, so we thought we'd come down here and skip stones. We must have fallen asleep. I'm sorry we scared you."

Donald did not realize the children had overheard them arguing, and he felt bad for it.

20

"That's okay boy. Come on let's get you two home."

As they walked away, both Starr and Billy turned back around trying to catch a glimpse of Celine or Tege. They could see nothing through the darkness.

Over time, they often wondered themselves if their adventure had been real or a dream.

Kova

July 14th, Southern California

After escaping Mom and her beloved chores, Karl rode his bicycle down the road in the back hills, which lay next to undeveloped land. As always, he brought his loyal companion and only true friend, Buck, a Labrador retriever. Buck was trained in the best school his father could afford. They had developed a special bond; it was as though Buck knew Karl's commands before he gave them.

About a half hour into their ride, the sunset and darkness settled in, bringing a sudden chill to the air. As they topped a hill, Karl could see a faint glow in the wooded ravine below with some people gathered around it. His friend Timmy had told him tales of witchcraft and animal sacrifices being practiced in these hills. Although he believed in none of this, he was curious. He hid his bicycle in the bushes at the side of the road to investigate this unusual gathering. Quietly, Karl and his dog crept into the wooded area towards a campfire.

When they came to the edge of the wooded area, Buck darted out towards the people standing around the fire. Karl watched in dismay as his dog lunged at one of them. Fearing these strange robed beings might see him, Karl hid behind a tree. As he did, he heard a sharp, painful yelp emanate from his beloved dog. Certain Buck had met with an early demise he stood frozen in fear. Then he could hear muffled voices closing in on him, and a panic rushed through his body. Gathering all his strength inside, he frantically ran back towards the road as fast as he could but the hypnotic sound of the chanting voices grew ever closer. An unholy presence brushed against him, then rushed past, and swirled around him. He stopped, fearfully hoping to catch a glimpse of what might be touching him. As he did so, there was a rustle in the grass, which was racing towards him. Something dark and ominous was about to overtake him. Suddenly, Buck flew out of nowhere, growling as a mad dog. Knocking him to the ground, Buck viciously tore at Karl's face. He desperately struggled to unlock Buck's jaw from his face but the more Karl tried to push him away, the more fiercely Buck attacked him.

The sound of a police helicopter became louder, as it approached. Its blinding light shone on Karl's limp body, as he lay helplessly under Buck's deadly grip. A shot rung out and Buck laid limp and heavy on Karl's chest. Two police officers ran to assist Karl and to make sure the dog was dead. Buck was most definitely dead, but this did not loosen his grip on Karl. One officer had to break the animal's jaw, to free Karl.

Karl had gone into shock. His face an ashen white stained with blood, his right eye missing. His other eye stared straight up, searching the skies for the dark movement that had descended upon him. The officer leaned over Karl, checking his pulse. As he did he noticed Karl mouthing words, so he leaned down close to hear what he was saying. Karl attempted to speak, again. In a weak, whisper Karl said, "They have come.... to steal our souls."

December 31st, La Grange, Georgia

Driving to the church for the grand New Years celebration, Anna pondered Pastor Littlejohn's last sermon. His words greatly perplexed her. He kept talking about "the day of the Lord was at hand." How God had revealed to him, through some hidden numerology, the day of his return. No matter how she had crunched the numbers, she never came close to his calculations. In fact, the number she kept coming up with was 12,436. So deep in this thought, she was startled when her cell phone rang. She fumbled around in her purse to retrieve it.

"Hello? Ray ...yeah...what? What are you talking about? Yes, I have my bible with me. Hold on a second let me pull over."

She drove her SUV over to the side of the road, picked up her bible as she spoke back into the phone.

"Now you said what? 1.24.36 could only mean Matthew, the first book of the New Testament, chapter 24 verse 36. Yeah, I'm turning to it. Why this verse and not some other verse? Yes, yes, I've got it. It says, 'No one knows about the day or hour, not even the angels in heaven, nor the Son, but only the Father.' Oh, my God, if you're right, what in God's name is Pastor Littlejohn planning. My husband and my daughter are there."

Anna threw the phone down on the passenger's seat, slammed her car into drive, and then sped down the highway.

It was just a few minutes before midnight. Pastor Littlejohn had brought the congregation to a heightened frenzy of "hallelujah's," and "amen's." Standing behind the pulpit, he lifted his hands in praise. Loudly he proclaimed, "The day of the Lord is at hand. The end times are upon us. Oh Lord, how we have waited patiently for your return." As he spoke, the ushers closed the wood shutters covering the stain glass windows, placing a metal bar across them. Simultaneously, a bar locked into place at the entry doors.

"Be not frightened my children for soon we will be absent from the body and present with the Lord."

An eerie silence came over the congregation. Jonathan picked up his daughter, holding her tightly in his arms. Little Lisa whimpered in his arms. "I'm scared Daddy." He looked around at the other scared and confused faces. Terror filled his whole being, as the ushers took small canisters from under their robes. They snapped the rings off the tops and red smoke filled the air. As they dropped them to the floor, screams, choking coughs and gasping for air are heard. Most of the congregation rushed the doors, to no avail. Pastor Littlejohn took a flare, lit it, and then threw it down the center aisle. Jonathan watched as though his life was moving in slow motion. He stared in disbelief at this man he had trusted for these past three years. As he looked upon his face, he saw a strange transformation. No longer did he see the face of a man, but of an evil being who was delighted with what he had done. Then in a blink of an eye, Pastor Littlejohn and his henchmen were gone.

Anna pulled up to the church to hear screaming coming from within. She ran to the front door, pulling on them with all her might.

"Jonathan! Lisa! Jonathan!" She yelled.

An explosion rocked the building from inside, blasting the stain glass windows out and knocking Anna from the steps onto the ground. Covering her head with her hands, she laid there momentarily until she realized she was unharmed. Determined to rescue her husband and daughter, she stood only to see the church engulfed in flames. Dropping to her knees she screamed, "No, dear God, no, no, no," then fell prone on the ground sobbing.

Anna, engulfed in her own grief, was not even aware of the emergency crews arrival. Busy with containing the blaze, they did not notice Anna still laying prone in the grass, sobbing and mumbling. Cadet Higgins nearly stepped on her as he brought a fire hose around to the front of the burning church.

"Sarge, there's a survivor over here," He shouted.

He stooped over Anna's sobbing form.

"Lady, are you okay? Are you hurt? Do you need medical help? Here, let me help you up."

Higgins set the hose down, in order help Anna to her feet. As he did, he noticed blood coming from her hands. Sergeant Adams approached them, also noting her wounds.

"Medic, we need a medic. Someone bring a blanket. Higgins, what's she saying?"

Anna stared blankly at the flames. Higgins looked at her, the flames, then turned to Sergeant Adams.

"It sounds like, have mercy on their souls, no one knows the day or the hour. She just keeps saying it over and over. What does it mean, Sir?"

"Maybe it means she's the crazy who set this fire," He said coldly.

January 22nd, Gowanda, New York

During the budget cutbacks in the 80's, a large mental institution run by the state closed down. The Kova Research Institute, a private corporation, bought Gowanda State Hospital. They continued to take mental patients, at least for those whose families could afford to pay, who were willing to agree to the experimental treatments. Since those who were admitted were considered incurable, their families were more than willing to sign any documents set before them.

Mr. and Mrs. Kinzel entered the director's plush office. Dr. Evan Lantz stood, extending his hand to Mr. Kinzel.

"Please sit. I just want to take this time to assure you that your daughter will receive the best care we have available. We have had great success in treating schizophrenia with a new drug we developed."

Mrs. Kinzel, concerned for her daughter's physical health as well as mental recovery, needed to know more than what the brochures in her hand had to say.

"Tell me more about this new drug Dr. Lantz," She requested.

He leaned forward and placed his hand on a sealed glass domed jar.

"As you know, Dr. Kova discovered a new plant, whose seed lay in meteorites he found in Death Valley. The seed was brought here and cultivated. The plant held in this jar is called Kova."

Mrs. Kinzel nervously sat back in her chair. She stared at the thistle like plant with a blood red bloom.

"I heard it is very poisonous."

"I understand your concern. It is really a very simple process to make the plant's poisonous attributes inert. We then discovered it had an amazing ability to restore the synapses of the brain. Therefore, it allows the patient to respond to therapy. Come let me show you around so you will feel confident with the care we provide."

They both nodded their heads in compliance. Mr. Kinzel stood and spoke for the first time. "You know they thought my daughter was responsible for the fire. I know my daughter. She could never have done anything so heinous."

Evan placed his arm around the old man. "None of that matter's here, Mr. Kinzel, we promise to make her better. That's what you want, isn't it? You want your little girl back, yes?" He reached over to press a button on the intercom. "Marge, have Hank secure the day room. We are bringing a new guest in with her parents. Understood?"

"Understood Dr. Lantz." Marge responded.

Hank, a twenty-three year old orderly, entered the day room. Hank had great hopes of becoming a pro-baseball player, like his namesake. Unfortunately, while he was a rookie with the minors, he broke his collarbone and developed Raynaud's disease in his right hand. His pitching career was over quicker than it began. His mother, an RN, found him a job with the hospital. He discovered he had a special talent for dealing with the mentally ill, having a calming effect on them. Hank knew exactly what securing the day room meant. He walked directly over to a thin little boy huddled in a corner rocking back and forth. The disheveled looking boy had horrible scars running down the right side of his face. Hank squatted down in front of him, placing his hands on the kid's shoulders to stop him from rocking.

"Now Karl, Karl look at me. Stop the mumbling, just for a moment. Okay?"

Karl stopped for a moment, peering deep into Hank's face. "They've come to steal our souls, Hank. They are all around us. Don't you see them?"

"You poor tormented soul, no Karl, I don't see them... Karl my friend, I need you to do something for me. Are you hearing me Karl?"

Karl did his best to focus on Hank's words. "Yes, Hank I hear you?"

"We are receiving a new guest. I need you to behave like a gentleman. Please, try to keep the demon thing to yourself. It scares the newcomer's. I'll be right here with you when they come in. Nobody is going to hurt you when I'm here. You know that, don't you Karl?"

Karl glared deeply into Hanks face again. "Nope, no demons with you. You can stay. I'll behave, promise."

"That's my good little buddy."

Hank and Karl were sitting at a table playing checkers, when Dr. Lantz with his guests entered the day room. The room was orderly; the people were calm and lucid except for Karl, who was nervously trying to catch a glimpse of the newcomer. Mrs. Kinzel had hold of Anna's arm, directing her through the room. Anna stopped and tilted her head skyward with her arms slightly bent and her hands held outward. She looked like a statue of 'Christ', Karl had seen. He bolted out of his chair, nearly knocking Dr. Lantz down. He grabbed a chair and placed it directly in front of Anna. Standing inches from Anna's face, he stared deeply into her eyes. Karl smiled as he looked upon Anna, who was unresponsive.

"She is a protected one. No demon can have this one," He stated as a matter of fact.

Karl took Anna's hand and kissed it. Anna moaned, then the palm of her hand started to bleed and tears ran down her face.

Red faced, Dr. Lantz could hardly control his anger.

"Hank, Get this, this... Get him out of here."

Once Karl was restrained, Dr Lantz marched over to him. "For this you get an extra treatment tonight."

Terror filled Karl's face. "No, no, please no. I promise to do better. Please don't..."

Two very large men dragged him out of the day room kicking and screaming. "Let go of me, demons. I demand you, let go of me."

Dr. Lantz quickly composed himself. "Mr. and Mrs. Kinzel, I am very sorry you had to witness this. Unfortunately, we don't have a one hundred percent success rate yet, but we are working on it."

Mrs. Kinzel was wiping Anna's hands with her handkerchief. "It's the first time since the night of the fire she has responded to anything, but why did her hands start to bleed? It's been under control for weeks."

Dr. Lantz still irritated from the current events responded, "That boy has an uncanny ability to disrupt the most tranquil of moments. It won't happen again. This I can assure you."

The next morning, Hank stopped in to have his morning visit with Karl. He was understandably confused when he found Karl's bed empty. He immediately ventured to the nurse's station to inquire as to Karl's whereabouts. Nurse Knapp, a middle aged woman, took out Karl's chart, reading it, she informed Hank of the patient's location. "It appears they have moved him to building J. Dr. Chen's notes indicate that the patient is unresponsive to current treatment. He is also disruptive and a danger to other patients."

Hank grabbed the chart out of the nurse's hand to read it for himself. "This is bull. It says here he attacked another patient wounding her. That woman has that stigmata thing. Who knows what would make her bleed. Jeesh! Where the heck is this building J? I've never heard of it."

Nurse Knapp snatched the chart out of Hank's hand. "It's in the same building as the research lab, but they won't let you in there. You don't have clearance."

"What do they do over there? How many patients are there? What kind of treatment are they getting there?" Hank questioned.

Nurse Knapp held up her hands to stop his one breath questionnaire. "Hold on there. They don't tell and frankly, I don't ask. I just do my job. So should you, if you want to keep yours. Now, they have scheduled you to be Anna's full-time escort while she adjusts to life on the ward. So be a good little orderly and make sure she eats her breakfast."

Disappointed, Hank acknowledged his new assignment, "All right, but damn, I really liked Karl, demons n'all. Could you do me a favor? Ask if I could be allowed to visit him?"

Nurse Knapp liked Hank, she warmly responded, "I'll ask, but I don't guarantee anything."

Hank leaned over and gave her a kiss on the cheek. "You're the best."

Nurse Knapp shook her head and smiled, "Kisses, and flattery? The next thing I know, you'll be bringing me flowers and candy. I already said I'd ask. You save all this mooshy stuff for your girlfriend."

"Don't have one." Hank said as he was walking away.

"Well you need to get a life outside of this place!" Nurse Knapp yelled at the back of his head.

"Yeah, I know. My mom says the same thing." He responded then disappeared around the corner.

Nurse Knapp wrote something down in a file, closed it and placed it in a wire basket on the counter. She stared down the hall where she last saw Hank. "Well, your mama is right young man. You don't get a life outside of this hellhole, you'll end up just like them and wouldn't that be a sorry sight to see. God help us all." She mumbled to herself.

Hank had been at Anna's side all day and she did not once respond to him. On warm days, the patients were allowed to spend time in the courtyard. Hank and Anna strolled down a tree-lined path when Anna abruptly stopped. She turned towards the lab, and pointed. Hank elated at her attempt to communicate asked, "What? What are you trying to say, Anna?"

For the first time in almost a month, she spoke, "There, go there."

"No, I'm sorry we can't go there. Why do you want to go there, Anna?"

She closed her eyes as though she was trying to sense something. "Karl, they're hurting Karl."

Hank was completely puzzled by Anna's remarks. "Karl? How do you know they are hurting him?"

For the first time she looked into Hank's face. "I know, I just know."

At the end of Hank's shift, he stopped by the nurse's station.

"Is Nurse Knapp here?"

A young female nurse looked up from her work.

"No, she left early, Dr.'s appointment. Are you, Hank?"

He smiled flirtatiously, "That's not fair, you know my name and I don't know yours."

She pointed to her ring finger, which was donning a wedding band. "Cute, nice try. Here, Nurse Knapp left you an envelope. She said you're on your own with this one. Do you know what she meant?"

Hank took the envelope and snuck a quick look inside. There he found an entry card to the lab. "Yeah, I know. Thanks." He read her nametag. "Rita."

Hank placed the card in his pant pocket and departed.

While in the locker room, Hank found a white jacket in the dirty garment hamper, which mistakenly had Dr. Robert's name tag left on it. He put the jacket on then strolled over to the entry door of building J. He slid the card through the access panel; the door opened. Trying to look as though he belonged there, he walked straight to the main station. The night crew was limited to an emergency staff of one. Fortunately, no one was there, so Hank helped himself to the chart rack. Locating Karl's chart, he read it over. "Karl Kemp, room one-oh-eight. Eight A.M. / total reprogramming. Total reprogramming! What the heck does that mean?"

Quickly he marched down the hall to find room 108. As he walked down the corridor, he peered into each room to find most of them empty. The few patients, he did see, were restrained to their beds. He ventured about half way down the hall to Karl's room to find his little body strapped to his bed. The light over his bed was off. The television was on, but it displayed nothing but static. Hank walked over to Karl and gently shook his shoulder.

"How are you doing, my little friend?"

There was no response. Karl stared at the television with his one good eye. It was as though there was nothing left of the child he once knew.

"My God, what did they do to you?"

Out of the corner of his eye, Hank noticed a movement. He turned to see Anna standing in the doorway. "You scared me half to death. What are you doing here?"

Anna walked over to Karl and placed her hands on him, one on his forehead and one on his chest. "They've come to steal our souls." She said as she closed her eyes and tilted her head toward the ceiling. Karl blinked, and then focused in on their faces.

"Help us Hank. Help us get out of here." Karl begged.

"Please Hank, help us to leave this evil place." Anna pleaded.

Hank undid the straps to Karl's arms and legs. "I must be crazy. I'll lose my job for this. Anna you still haven't told me what you're doing here."

"God's will." Anna stated in a calm and knowing voice.

Hank shook his head. "That's not the answer I was looking for. Damn, ask a crazy person a question, get a crazy answer. Hell, I don't know where we think we are going, much less how to get there."

All three proceeded to walk towards the entry doors. A door opened behind them and a large man stepped out of the men's room.

"Hey, where do you think your going? Come back here?" He yelled.

Hank, Anna and Karl kept walking, ignoring him.

"STOP!" He barked.

Karl broke out in a full run with Anna and Hank at his heels. Just as they reached the main station, a man stepped out from around the nurse's station causing them to slide to a stop.

"Well, hello Anna. We missed you at services."

Anna glared at the man before her. Pastor Littlejohn smiled as the large man boxed them in from the other side.

"It's time for your conversion," Pastor Littlejohn said.

Anna stepped toward him defiantly. "I'm not afraid of you. You have no power over me."

Anger, hate, and disgust drained the Pastor's face of all humanity. He stepped forward grabbing her arm. Anna's hands immediately started to bleed. She yanked her arm away and blood from her wounds trickled onto Pastor Littlejohn's skin. A look of disbelief was on his face as he grabbed his hand in agonizing pain. His skin started to smolder. He gasped for air, to find none. There was the appearance of something moving under his skin, on his face and hands. Then the skin peeled away leaving a grotesque image of a demon like face as his whole body burst into flames.

Karl looked at Hank. "I told you they were demons."

Anna turned to the large man, raising her hands, which were still dripping of blood. The man backed away. She headed toward the door. "We must go now." Hank and Karl followed her to the door. Karl pulled out his card, but before he could enter it into the pad, the door opened.

The large man made one more attempt towards them. Anna waved her hand to sprinkle her blood across his chest. He fell back, grabbing his chest, writhing in pain.

As they exited the building, the door slammed shut behind them.

At the front gate of the institution, there was an old beat up Chevy waiting with the motor running. Nurse Knapp opened the door. "Come, it's time to go."

An explosion rocked the ground. Hank turned to see a bright light with a strange blue green hue, coming from behind the main building, building J. He headed towards the car then stopped, staring at Anna. "Who are you people? Who, what were they? What in God's name is going on here?"

Anna placed her hand on his face and he pulled back in fear.

"You have no need to be afraid. We cannot hurt you. Some may say we are messengers, warriors for God. Perhaps we were just given the gift to see, expose, and yes, destroy. Where they came from, I don't know. Demons? Hmm, wouldn't you say anything that comes to destroy mankind is evil?"

Hank was not sure he liked or understood Anna's answer. He stepped towards the car and gazed up at the night sky. A meteor darted across the sky then another and another. Before long, the sky was showered with falling lights.

Beware of wolves in sheep's clothing. For what appears in the name of God, may not be of God at all.

Forever & Ever, Amen

      Walking into the kitchen, Richard threw his car keys down on the counter. He draped his plaid flannel jacket over the breakfast nook chair and set his gloves atop the jacket. Quinn, his five-year-old daughter, the love of his life, was at Bud and Amy's house for their daughter Stacey's seventh birthday party. Quinn would be gone all afternoon. She was ecstatic. Richard was none too sad about it either; this was the first time he could remember since they moved there that he had the place all to himself. He reveled in the silence. The thought of an uninterrupted cup of hot tea appealed to him. He shook the teapot to see if it contained enough water for a cup. It did. He turned the knob to high. No flame. The pilot light had gone out again. One of these days, he thought he would actually get the thing fixed. Taking a match from a small ceramic jar that sat on top of the stove, (for just such occasions) he struck it against the wall, leaving a mark aside several other marks. He poked the match under the pot, which exploded, singeing the hairs on his hand. "Damn," he spit, "Stupid, stupid, stupid, when the hell well I ever learn."

Running cold water over his hand, he noticed a faint powdery sweet smell, almost like candy. He brought his hand to his nose. Nope, it wasn't him. From his hand, all he could detect was the smell of burnt hair. Yet, it was so familiar but for the life of him, he could not place from where. Dismissing it from his mind, he went to the hall closet to locate a box of books he had yet to unpack since the move. He knew in one of these boxes had to be the book he had been looking for. He had started it years ago but had never found the time to finish it. He was notorious for starting books and never finishing them. Considering the turmoil in his life these past six years, he felt he had a better excuse than most.

Setting the box down by his easy chair, he wandered over to the living room window. The house was an A frame chalet built in the 70's. He loved the floor to ceiling windows that faced Cayuga Lake. There were no storm clouds in the sky, and the sun shone down on the lake. The lake was calm and smooth. The local trees had started to turn. Hints of red and yellow were replacing the lush green of the hillside. Bud had told him he could not remember a Christmas without snow on the ground. Yet, to Richard it looked as though it were eighty degrees outside. Only he knew better, because he just came in from the bitter cold. There was to be no Indian summer this year. As he stared out the window, he saw one die-hard fisherman sitting in his johnboat about fifty yards from the shoreline. He thought maybe next summer he and Quinn would do a little fishing, if he could get her to sit still long enough.

40

A whistle screamed from his teapot, diverting his attention from this moment of pure escapism. He took a box of teabags from the cupboard to place a bag in his cup and noted there was already one waiting for the steaming water from his pot. Odd, he didn't remember taking it out. Again, there was that faint smell he could not place. Not to be dissuaded from a few hours of peace and quite, he again dismissed these strange little instances as his own lapses of memory and settled into his chair. He set the box on his lap and took a small sip of tea, realizing he forgot to add honey. Honey made the tea not the exotic blends sold at the local health food store. As he was about to remedy this error, he found his book. He placed the box back down on the floor and opened the book to the cover page. Inside was an inscription from Tanya. It read: To my husband, my lover, and my friend. Happy Birthday. Tanya. A flash of cynicism poured out. "Yeah, right. Like that was ever the case." He turned the page to find a picture of the two of them when they had first fallen in love.

It was a short courtship, full of passion. They never could seem to get enough of each other. His friend Adam said, "You guys better get married cuz you'll never survive this dating stuff, if you know what I mean?"

Richard thought that was a strange remark and asked why he would say such a thing. Al's response was one of profound wisdom and knowledge.

"Because once you're married you'll be lucky if you get some once a month."

***

Richard had been hired straight out of college by Fotodak in Brockport, New York, to head product design. Film developing by and large was dropping to the wayside to self-printing, due to the advent of the digital cameras. Even though Fotodak had diversified its product line, it needed to maintain its corner of the picture-making and producing market. Foreign industries were flooding the market place with digital everything. The cameras were pricey, and Fotodak was looking for a way to produce cameras of equal or superior quality at a reduced price. Richard was one of the most sought after designers in the country. His doctoral thesis was a design of high digital storage combined with low energy use. Two patents came out of his thesis, and Fotodak bought the rights. Richard was part of the package. The financial compensation would allow him to pay off his student loans and buy a house in less than two years.

Adam Lamb was the director of marketing. Richard reported directly to this tall, skinny, over caffeinated man. When it came to the details of the business, Adam knew all there was to know and then some. He was a boy genius, who had made his mark in the industry two years before Richard had graduated. They hit it off immediately. Although sometimes he was a little more blunt than he was accustomed to, Richard liked his no-nonsense, get to the bottom line approach.

Adam and Richard had just finished their lunch at Hanley's, an upscale restaurant used almost exclusively for entertaining prospective clients. Adam, in a usual state of calm, ordered a double espresso and a cappuccino, then mixed the two drinks together. Richard had his usual, a diet coke. He pulled a bound presentation from his briefcase so Adam could review it and make suggestions for the up coming meeting and discuss the marketing strategy for some of Richard's new product designs. Adam was babbling on and on about demographics and his statistical analysis, but Richard was not paying him a bit of attention. He was captivated by a woman being seated by the maître d'. Adam realizing he had been talking to himself twisted around to observe what had Richard so entranced.

"Ah…Plain Jane Tanya." He said.

"Plain Jane Tanya, why in the world would you say that? She has to be the most beautiful woman I have ever seen."

His eyes were still glued to this statuesque figure sitting across the room from him. She was wearing a gray suit, the jacket-skirt kind, with a collarless blouse. Her dark blonde hair was pulled back into a French braid. Her high cheekbones, long slender legs, combined with the grace and poise of a ballerina, were more the stuff of a glamour model than a plain Jane. Her demeanor was sophisticated, aloof, and professional. She certainly was not Richard's image of 'Plain Jane.'

"Well that's what we called her in High School," Adam said.

"You knew her, you know her?"

"Yeah, we went to the same school, upstate. Graduating class of maybe two hundred and fifty. We all had nick names. They called me whiz kid or hoops."

"I understand whiz kid, but hoops?"

Adam preferred to tout his athletic abilities over his intellect. He hated the geek category.

"I had two interests, mathematics and basketball. I could dunk the ball from just about anywhere on the court. I was even better if I had a running start. Come on, you mean to tell me they didn't have nicknames for everyone in your school?"

"Um, my graduating class was more like twelve hundred. If you weren't part of the athletic elite you weren't even noticed."

"Ah, come on. A tall good-looking guy like yourself must have had women hanging all over you, and with your build, you had to have played sports."

"Chess."

"Richard, that's not a sport."

"I know. I never cared for organized brutality. I did play golf in my senior year. I wasn't bad, but I wasn't good either."

"Golf, I suppose that does qualify as a sport. Sorta."

"In college I did racquet ball and karate. I guess I liked the one on one stuff better."

"Alright, now you're doing better and they called me a geek. I figured you to have been the jock with women clamoring all over you."

"Ooo, not hardly, not hardly. I had my nose in the books bound and determine to do better than my old man. He lived paycheck to paycheck until the day he died and I was going to be a success. I was going to college, and I was going to be filthy rich."

"I'd say at this rate, you're well on your way to that goal."

Richard, unlike most men he knew, really did not like to talk about himself. He found himself gazing back over in Tanya's direction. This time she was aware of his stare. She smiled, then summoned the waiter over. Richard found that the palms of his hands were sweating. He had to know more.

"Now, back to 'Plain Jane Tanya'. Why did they call her that?"

"As far as I can remember, she was what they called a wallflower. Like you, always had her head crammed in some book. I don't remember her having any friends. She was pretty much a loner. Actually, I'm surprised we even noticed her long enough to give her a nick name"

"Well," Richard said clearing his throat. "She certainly has blossomed. Can you, will you introduce me to her?"

Adam leaned forward, hovering over his cappuccino with a grin on his face. He signaled Richard to come in closer. Then in almost a whisper he says, "That'll be real easy. I'll introduce you at the staff meeting."

"Staff meeting? You mean she works with us?"

"Yep."

"Where, what division?"

"Dang, you haven't even met her yet and she already has you wrapped around her little finger. She works in advertising and I'd say you both have that something special in common."

"And, what's that."

"You are both driven by your need to be successful and as you so eloquently stated before, 'become filthy rich.'"

Tanya was exactly that, driven. She was working her way up the corporate hierarchy in the advertising department, determined to be a CEO or head of the board of directors before she was forty. Her personal policies were no serious relationships and never ever date anyone you work with. All of that changed at the staff meeting.

Adam started the meeting with an outline of all the items to be addressed. The next four hours included an hour and a half of Richard's product designs. This included cameras, starting with 100 giga bites of storage, zoom lenses, and digital video cameras, all with a competitive price tag. He introduced high definition printers which were strictly designed to print pictures from the storage disks with proprietary ink cartridges, to insure reoccurring orders. Last but not least, there was paper, glossy, matte, canvas, and picture printable bond paper. Richard had a knack of making the mundane interesting, if not down right exciting. Using all his charm, wit and off beat humor, his time at center front flew by. This was his best performance ever, and the underlying beat was all directed to woo Tanya. It worked. Every time their eyes met, little sparks of sexual magnetism filled the air. It appeared Adam was the only outsider who noticed. He almost burst out laughing when he finally introduced them.

They married three months later. Adam was the best man and a woman from the typing pool stood as the matron of honor. Tanya knew her only as a daily acquaintance, but she was the closest thing to a friend Tanya had. This should have been a huge warning sign for Richard, but he was too much in love to see it. Tanya did not allow women close, they were a threat, and men were to be competed against. It didn't take long for the veil over his eyes to be lifted.

It had only been about four months since they had taken their wedding vows. Richard was still high on the honeymoon faze of their marriage. He was walking out of the break room, coffee in hand, talking to an attractive young lady from engineering. Her eyes sparkled with excitement as she told him how her fiancée had just called to tell her he had obtained tickets to the Randy Travis concert. Tanya had turned the corner just in time to see their smiling faces. She seethed with jealousy. Her face turned ugly with anger and suspicion. Throwing her head up and her shoulders back, Tanya marched over to Richard as the young woman left.

"Who was that?"

"Hi Hon."

"Don't Hi Hon me, tell me who that was."

Richard was taken back by the tone in her voice.

"Sara, she works in engineering. What's going on? Why are you so hostile?"

"What's going on? That's what I'd like to know, Dick. What were you two planning? A little soiree while I'm out of town on business next week? Huh, DICK?"

This was so far off the mark of anything Richard would ever consider. He stood staring at her in complete disbelief at the words coming out of her mouth. It was also the first time she had referred to him, as Dick. She had said it with such venom and distain. He knew the truth would seem too trite for her to believe so he made up a lie in order to keep the peace. His first lie in what became a lifestyle, all for the sake of peace.

"No, hon. I heard that Randy Travis was going to be performing locally and she's a big fan. I figured she'd know if the concert is sold out and if tickets were still available. I just wanted us to have a nice night out on the town. We haven't taken any time for ourselves lately. That's all. I just wanted some special time with my woman."

Richard caressed her cheek with his hand and smiled. He loved this woman, he lived and breathed for this woman, and now he prayed she bought his lie.

"Oh, yes, I'd like that. Just let me know the date and time so I can write it down in my calendar." Tanya's voice toned down to calm and professional, there was no warmth but happily there was no hostility.

"I will." Richard said, trying not to show his own perplexity.

"Good, I'll see you later then." She stepped up and gave him a quick kiss on his cheek then disappeared down the hall.

Richard stood rubbing his head as though he had just been slammed by a two by four. Tanya had bought the lie but the matter of fact way in which she had responded was uncanny. He spent the next day and a half making calls to obtain tickets to a sold out concert. He did. They were scalped at $250 a pop, but he had tickets.

Their work schedules did not leave much togetherness time. Even when they were home they were laboring on work related projects. So, the concert was a needed break for them. He made sure it was a very special night for Tanya. There were flowers, dinner, the concert and wine n' cheese in front of a roaring fire at the end of the night. The night of the concert was reminiscent of their early courtship. Their lovemaking was as passionate as ever. It all reminded Richard, why he fell in love with Tanya in the first place.

***

Three weeks later the hammer dropped. Tanya was pregnant and it did not sit well with her at all. She had morning sickness from the time she got up until the time she went to bed. She spent more time at home in bed or hugging the porcelain god than she did at work. Her work was the only thing that made her feel important, useful. She missed it with every fiber of her being. As much as Richard loved her, he could hardly stand to go home at night. Tanya did not change out of her PJ's, and fixing her hair or putting on makeup was a thing of the past. She started criticizing everything he did. No matter what he did, when he did it, it was never good enough or at the right time. He almost could tolerate the constant biting in her voice. It was just when it was combined with her jealousy he thought he would go mad.

Richard had a long talk with Al and managed to convince him to let her work on some advertising projects at home. Al could pay her for piecework, pro bono if necessary, anything to distract her from watching Richard's every move. With the morning sickness abating a little and the distraction of working on her advertising designs, she seemed content. When he came home at night, she seemed almost chipper. Tanya would greet him with a hug and a kiss. The woman he knew and loved was back. She even tried to be romantic in her own clumsy way. The timer on the stereo would click on at six ten every night, just about the time Richard walked through the door, and every night it played a particular song off the CD they had purchased at the concert. Before he had his coat hung in the closet, the first verse of "Forever & Ever, Amen" by Randy Travis was blaring over the speakers. It was sweet at first but it started to grate on his nerves. She had it set to loop so it played over and over and over. He found he could not bring himself to say anything about it. She knew this too. There were times she would put the recording on merely to taunt him.

Life continued as well as could be expected with a pregnant woman in the house, although Richard was concerned about the number of hours Tanya worked on her projects. She was obsessed with maintaining her visibility in the advertising world. Fearing if she were too long out of the limelight, she would be starting from ground zero again.

Then complications with the pregnancy set in. Richard thought it was because she wasn't eating correctly. Sometimes, he noted, she consumed no more than a bagel and tea for the entire day. It was more than her body could handle. He came home one evening to find her passed out on the bathroom floor.

The next morning, Richard went to the hospital. The doctor flagged him down as he was about to enter her room with a beautiful bouquet of flowers. Dr. Siegel ushered him away from Tanya's room towards the nurse's station.

"Mr. Pelling, your wife and the baby are stable. She's a lucky lady. Had you been even an hour later I'm afraid we would not be having this conversation. Mr. Pelling, I am very concerned about your wife's and baby's health. Are you aware that she is taking illegal drugs?"

"What do you mean illegal drugs? What kind of drugs?"

"I had blood and urine taken last night and had it rushed to the lab because of what I suspected. The lab found methamphetamines. I followed up with a visual this morning, it appears she has been snorting it because her sinus passages are very inflamed, and now she is showing signs of withdrawal. If we don't get this under control right now, she will lose the baby and frankly I am very concerned about the damage she may have already done. Her own health is already in jeopardy, and she is refusing to allow me to do more tests. So, unless you can convince her of allowing further testing on the baby, I'm afraid I'll have to pursue a court order. "

"Sweet Jesus, I didn't know. I knew she was staying up too late, and she complained of allergies, but I didn't know. How could I have been so blind?"

"Addicts have a way of hiding these things. In fact they are known for going to extraordinary measures to make sure no one knows. Extreme mood changes can be a good indicator, but we are dealing with a pregnant woman. So, all bets are off there."

"Addict, you're saying she's an addict?"

"Yes, I'd say she has been doing this most of her adult life. That's why I say her health is in jeopardy. She has a heart murmur which she probably has had all her life. The amphetamines jump-starting her heart on a regular basis has weakened it as well as lowered her immune system. She also has complications stemming from the pregnancy. She has what is commonly referred to pregnancy-induced diabetes. Under normal conditions, we restrict the diet and test her blood for sugar, but as you can see these are not normal conditions. If this behavior were to continue, I fear she would lose the baby or its birth weight and development would be greatly compromised. So far the baby's birth weight appears normal and the development appears normal, but I need further tests to be sure. Therefore, I would like you to consent to a minimum of two weeks hospitalization so we can get your wife and the baby healthy. Then once she's home, she needs to be confined to bed rest for the duration. We can provide counseling for the addiction, but it is all up to her if she stays clean. I must stress that you need to get your wife to agree to all of this. Otherwise, I will go the way of the courts to protect the child."

"Of course, I'll do what ever is necessary. Is it alright if I go see her now? I think we have a lot to talk about."

"Yeah, only Mr. Pelling… I would prefer you not say anything about the drug addiction at this time. I would like someone from re-hab to talk to her first then we can do an intervention. Okay?"

"Thank you, Dr. Siegel. Thank you for being upfront about all of this. I'll abide by what ever you think it best. "

Tanya appeared to be asleep, so he took her water pitcher and set the flowers in it. The curtains were open, and the room filled with the morning light. Even without makeup, he thought she was beautiful. Concerned that the light would disrupt her sleep, he reached over to shut the curtains.

"Don't close them, I'm awake." Tanya said

"Hey beautiful, the woman of my dreams, the doctor says you're a lucky little girl, had I been an hour later, we could have lost the both of you. I thank God you and the baby are okay. Although he did said you have pregnancy induced diabetes, but with the right diet that can be easily controlled." Richard did his best to sound upbeat and hopeful.

He bent over to give her a kiss, and she deliberately turned her face away.

"Tanya, did you hear what I said? They said you and the baby are going to be just fine. You're just going to have to have bed rest for the duration of the pregnancy. That's all."

Tanya's head swung over, and her eyes flashed darts of anger at him. "That's all. That's all. I guess for you three months confined to a bed while this parasite sucks the life out of me is nothing."

"Tanya, let's not overreact. It's not like you're goin to be chained to the bed. You just have to take it real easy. This is your life and our child we are talking about. It's temporary, not forever."

"I had hoped I'd wake up with this thing inside me gone. It's not too late to have an abortion you know."

"Tanya, don't talk like that. I thought you wanted this baby. You acted so happy when you told me. God, if I had known, I would have never allowed this to happen. But it did. My God, this is a piece of you and me growing inside you. Our child, it's supposed to be a blessing. I...I... couldn't live with myself if I agreed to allow you to do that. I just couldn't live with myself."

"And you couldn't live with me either, could you?"

His eyes welled up with tears. All he could bring himself to say was, "No."

Tanya lay there taking long deliberate breaths trying not to cry. "I know you don't understand. So, I'll try my best to make you understand. My father told me all my life how it was all my fault that my mother was the way she was. That ever since my mother became pregnant with me, he had found her disgusting and my being born destroyed her body. He said she was a fat cow when she was pregnant and she remained a fat cow ever since. He refused to even touch her. Then to add insult to injury she had to go and have a girl, a plain Jane of a girl. He made it perfectly clear that no man would ever want such a homely thing like me. When I was sixteen he decided it was his fatherly duty to have me, since no other man would ever want me."

Tears ran down Richard's face as he kissed her hand.

"I'm so sorry. I...I...didn't know. Please understand I would never do anything to hurt you. I'll always love you, forever and ever." He smiled. "Just like that song says."

Richard spent every available moment he could at her side. While in the hospital, Tanya appeared to co-operate with the drug rehabilitation program.

In order to keep Tanya calm and happy, Richard found he had to rearrange his schedule. He bought a state of the art computer system that allowed him to use computer generated drafting and design programs. This would allow him to work out of the home. At home he could make sure she ate right and carried out her required exercise. Tanya liked the attention, plus she had control. She hated the time, limited as it was, that he had to go into the office. She would call him three or four times, on these short trips, to make sure he was not talking to other women. It drove him crazy. He would end up putting his cell phone on standby or turning it off completely, just so he could have an uninterrupted meeting with Adam. Of course, this was met with an inquisition when he arrived home.

Adam was concerned for Richard's sanity. Richard appeared tired and frazzled. He told him he was doing most of his work after Tanya had fallen asleep, it was the only way he could get anything of significance done. Adam decided to send him off to a seminar to learn a new software program they were installing at the office, which Richard would also need to install at home.

Richard arranged for a woman to come in three times a day to check on Tanya and to make sure she ate at regular intervals. Then he was off to M.I.T. for a week. Even with eight-hour classes' everyday, it was the most rest he had had in months. He called Tanya every night, and every night she cried about how lonely she was and how this woman he sent over was an incompetent boob. There were always questions about what women were in his class, who was he spending his time with after class. He found he didn't want to go home. When he finally did, he wished he hadn't.

Richard had been home for almost an hour, when Tanya went into a tirade about something. She screamed about his shoes being left in the middle of the floor, the ring left on the table from his iced tea, the pile of laundry by the washer, and his unpacked suitcase.

"Tanya, I'll take care of it. I'll take care of it all. Don't worry about it. You won't have to do a thing. Promise, I didn't leave it for you to do. Now, just calm down, it's not good for you."

"How would you know what's good for me, you haven't been here for a week. You don't know what I've been going through. Damn, with this mess you've made, I wish you hadn't come home. I wish your plane had gone down."

"Damn it Tanya, I know your miserable, but that's no reason to be a mean little bitch."

"What…you want me to act all sweet n'sugary like one of your little bimbos at the office?"

"Tanya, I am not seeing anyone at work. My god, how could I. I'm here practically twenty-four seven."

"Really, and what about little Sara in engineering?"

"What the hell are you talking about?"

"Sara, Sara is what the hell I am talking about. I called the office and found out little Miss Sara was also sent to that seminar. I've seen the way she looks at you, and you back. You bastard, you've probably been doing her through this entire pregnancy. Haven't you DICK. You pig."

Just as she said, "You pig" she took both her hands and shoved him in the chest, making him fall backwards over a chair and banging his head on the coffee table. Dazed and dismayed he sat up rubbing his hand over his head. His hand was covered in blood.

"Tanya, have you gone mad."

She stood there for a moment, feeling vindicated then almost as though she woke from a dream she gasped, "Oh my God Richard, I'm sorry. I didn't mean to do that. Let me go get some ice, or Band-Aids or something."

The next thing Richard heard was water running, the freezer door opening, then a groan. A sharp groan followed by a weak plea for help.

"Richard, the baby."

Richard jumped up to find her doubled over on the kitchen floor.

Quinn was born six hours later, three weeks early. Her birth weight was a little low; other than that, she was perfect. Richard talked to the doctor about Tanya's mood swings. Dr. Siegel had her screened for drugs. The test came out clean so he sent a psychiatrist to do an evaluation. Since Tanya had no intention of breast-feeding it was decided she would do well on antidepressants. It was also hoped this would circumvent the possibility of post partum depression. It helped.

They had a heck of a time finding the right formula for Quinn. Nobody slept. Besieged with bouts of colic, Quinn would scream for hours on end. Then after a well-baby checkup, the doctor sent them home with a case of formula designed for preemies. Finally, she slept for three-hour stints and so did the rest of the household, but Tanya was a nervous mother. Every time Tanya would pick up the baby, Quinn would cry. Richard was the only one who could calm her down. So, he spent the next three months at Tanya and Quinn's beck and call. As long as Richard was home with them, everything was fine. Tanya was loving and attentive. He didn't mind the diaper changing or the bottle feedings every few hours. This daddy business wasn't so bad; it had it's own rewards. Like the first time Quinn stopped sucking on her bottle to look up at him and gave him a milk drooling smile. Little Quinn had captured his heart in a manner he would have never thought possible.

Life seemed good for the next few years. The woman he loved was acting like a normal human being. He had a beautiful little girl who had him wrapped around her little finger, a job that not only paid well but was more than accommodating with his scheduling needs. Adam said they were the all American family with just a few minor glitches. Richard could live with that.

***

The day of Quinn's second birthday, they took her to Mousey Pizza House. All the noise and the mass of children running around made Tanya a nervous wreck. Being around a bunch of snot-nosed kids clinched a decision, she had been toying with for some time. Tanya announced she was going back to work.

"Hon, what about Quinn? I don't want to put her in some daycare where they could give a rat's behind about her. Have you thought about that?"

"Richard, my darling, you're already home ninety percent of the time. All we would have to do is hire someone to come to the house once or twice a week when you have to go into the office. Not much would change. I miss working, it was always very fulfilling. Anyway, you're a better mother than I could ever be."

When Tanya wanted or needed something she could be very endearing and persuasive. He acquiesced.

"When do you start?"

"Monday." Tanya said as a matter of fact.

"Monday?"

"Relax, I have faith in you, you'll work it out."

The transition went a lot smoother than Richard could have ever hoped for. The problem came when Tanya's new job demanded she travel. She was gone two weeks a month. The department store chain had originally hired her for advertising design then moved her to advertising sales. Later he found out, it was at her request. She had tired of sitting in an office day after day. She wanted to travel, see the world. The fighting started with a high pitch after she had come back home from a three-week trip of which the third week out was just for fun. Quinn hid behind Richard's leg and refused to go to her mother.

"What the hell is going on here Dick? You're turning my own daughter against me? What kind of nonsense are you filling her head with?"

"Damn it Tanya. You're gone fifty percent of the time, she barely recognizes you."

"I talk to her every night when I'm gone."

"It's not the same Tanya and you know it. She needs her mother here, not jetting across the country with an obligatory phone call here and there."

"Well, if you think I'm going to quit my job, you're full of it. She's just going to have to get used to it."

It had been almost a year since Tanya went back to work and every time she came home from a trip, they fought. Richard was not sure why he tried so hard to make the marriage work. His mother always said, "Marriage was for better or worse. No matter how difficult things got, you were supposed to make it work, find a way." Only he thought his father's perception fit better. His father liked to say, "A man who couldn't keep his woman was about as worthwhile as a dead horse in front of a plow." Richard supposed that concept was probably handed down from grandfather. It was the Pelling words of wisdom, words to live by. Divorce equaled failure.

The fighting escalated, what was once just screaming turned into a pushing match. She pushed he backed off. Her behavior became more and more erratic. Then one morning when he was helping her pack for the next trip, he discovered the cause. He was making sure she had a toothbrush and toothpaste (something she always managed to forget), when he found prescriptions, from several different doctors, for Valium and amphetamines. As she toweled off from her shower he held them out in his hand for her to see.

"What are these?"

"Exactly what they look like, and what are you doing snooping through my stuff anyway?"

"Why are you taking all this stuff?"

"Well moron, I have a hard time sleeping when I'm on the road, and my job demands a lot of energy and long hours. Therefore, these!"

She snatched them out of his hand and threw them into her makeup bag. It was obvious to Richard, there was going to be no more discussion on this subject. He joined Quinn in the kitchen. They giggled while coloring in her new baby animal coloring book, coloring the puppies green, blue, and rainbow striped.

"Here, use this one Daddy. Let's make a puple puppy. I want a puple one." Quinn insisted.

Tanya could hear their giggles from the bedroom while she dressed. It grated more on her nerves than that wretched Randy Travis song. Quinn had taken her place for Richard's affection. The two of them made her skin crawl and she couldn't wait to get out of there.

"Damn, it's too late to call a cab. Come on let's go before I miss my flight."

Tanya was habitually late. Richard grew to expect it and accept it, always working his schedule around her tardiness. She always had to look perfect before she left the house. Once upon a time, he saw this as an attribute; now it was a reminder of how self-absorbed she was. He saw her beauty as nothing more than vanity.

Quinn snuggled in her car seat in the back seat of the SUV, had fallen asleep minutes after the car started. The trip to the airport was stone quiet. They arrived with more than an hour to spare, due to the initial flight being canceled. The clerk apologized for the inconvenience and rebooked her on a different flight. All the airlines were having constant trouble with delays. There was no guarantee the next flight would take off as scheduled or be overbooked. He figured it all had to do with the increased security due to 9/11 and that was just the way it was.

They walked over in silence to check-in Tanya's luggage. Quinn pulled on her Richard's pant leg.

"Daddy, I'm hungry."

Richard trying not to rattle an already shaken cage, made the request as amicably as possible. These days he never knew what would set Tanya off.

"We've got time. How bout we all go get a bite to eat."

"You spoil her too much."

"How is feeding your child, spoiling her?"

"Never mind you wouldn't understand."

Richard threw up his hands in a motion of 'That's it, I surrender, and as he and Quinn headed for the cafeteria, Tanya followed. They all sat down at the only available table. Tanya could hardly sit still in her seat. Richard figured the amphetamines must have kicked in. Quinn picked and played with her food with disinterest.

"Daddy, I don't feel good."

"Come to mama sweetie. Let me see if you're running a temperature."

Tanya reached over to touch Quinn's forehead.

"Noooo!"

Quinn swatted at her mother's hand. This action set Tanya off, and she pushed away from the table knocking Quinn's chair over. Quinn hit the floor screaming her lungs out.

"See, see what you made me do. It's all your fault. If you hadn't made her such a daddy's girl, turned her against me this would have never happened." Tanya yelled and glared at Richard.

Tanya jumped up to retrieve Quinn from the floor. Richard had already done the same. Tanya shoved him back with all her strength. He fell back across the table behind him, spilling drinks and food over the people sitting there. He lunged forward to pull Quinn away from Tanya, fearful of what she might do. He was right to be afraid. Tanya held Quinn tight under her arms, while she kicked and screamed. When Tanya saw Richard come closer, she grabbed the only utensil left on the table, a fork.

"You come any closer I'll poke her eyes out. I swear to God, I'll poke her eyes out."

"Tanya please, put Quinn down. Just calm down, we can work this out."

"You're just like my father."

"What!"

"You heard me, you perverted bastard. You're just like my father. I should take her away from you before you do to her what he did to me."

"Tanya, I would never do that. You know I would never do that."

"I can't take the chance. You'll ruin her, just like he ruined me."

Every eye in the cafeteria was on Tanya. An older couple, whose table Richard had fallen on, were staring at her in horror.

"What you looking at old man. You want a piece of her too." Tanya snapped.

She looked around to see others gawking at her. To her right she detected a shadowy image approaching her. She swung Quinn and herself around.

"You. Get back. Stay away from me."

The young man complied without hesitation. Tanya moved the fork to Quinn's throat, with her eyes locked on Richard.

"Well DICK, I think I should do the merciful thing and spare this brat the agony of your affections."

Tanya pressed the fork against little Quinn's neck drawing blood. Quinn let out a high pitch, blood-curdling scream. Tanya forgot about the fork. She turned Quinn around, shaking her and screaming back.

"Stop it. Stop it I said. You stop with this incessant crying. I'm doing this for your own good."

Tanya stared at her daughter, seeing blood drip down her dress made a dramatic change in the tone of her voice. "Aw, poor thing, you're bleeding and you're ruining the new dress mommy bought you. Come let mommy clean you up."

She held Quinn close to her. Quinn did her best not to cry, taking deep panic-stricken breaths. Richard noticed a security guard sneaking up behind Tanya. The security guard grabbed both of Tanya's arms and pulled her down to a chair then pulled her arms back, releasing Quinn from her grip. Richard snatched his baby out of her lap as the security guard cuffed her hands behind the chair. It was all done in one swift move as though he had coordinated it with Richard.

Quinn's wound was superficial, but she had a heck of a time getting over the strep throat, which is why she didn't feel well in the first place. Tanya was placed in rehabilitation and much to Tanya's dismay was placed on a one-year probation for the incident. Richard's divorce lawyer insisted he file restraining orders against her and petition for full custody of his daughter. All was granted. He and Quinn moved to a town house in the suburbs. It was one of the few places he found that offered security that was to his satisfaction, just in case Tanya decided to find them. The house they had owned together went up for sale and for a little while Richard and Quinn's life settled down.

The house was taking forever to sell. He kept lowering the price hoping to get a taker. Alice, his real-estate broker, called him the day after he lowered it another thousand.

"Hi, Richard. This is Alice."

"I hope you have good news for me, Alice."

"Actually, knowing the troubles you've had lately, I was kind of concerned about the woman I just showed the house to."

"How's that?"

"Well, she seemed more interested in you than she was the house. She was asking questions like, where do you work, where did you move to, things like that. I just found it kind of odd. What did your ex-wife look like?"

"Oh my god, you don't think it was her do you?"

"I don't know. What does she look like?"

"She's about five eight, a hundred thirty pounds, blue eyes, with dark blonde hair. She is very striking to look at. Does that sound like your woman?"

"Damn, I thought if you described her I'd know but outside of the height, the rest is all wrong. This woman had red hair, which I know doesn't mean anything, and weighed more like ninety pounds sopping wet. She wore sunglasses, so I couldn't tell the eye color. Maybe she was just a nosey busybody, and there's nothing to worry about."

"Maybe, thanks Alice."

A couple of days later, Alice called again.

"I went to show the house again, but this time I had to call the police. It appears some kids had broken into the house and vandalized it.

"You sure it was kids?"

"Pretty sure. It looked like gang graffiti."

"How bad is it?"

"There's spray paint and long slices in the carpet. It's going to have to be replaced."

"All of it?"

"All of it. The wallpaper needs to be torn down. They slashed that all up and all of the walls will have to be sanded and repainted. There's black and red spray paint on every wall in the house. We might be able to save some of that beautiful oak trim but that's iffy. Fortunately, none of the appliances were destroyed. Maybe, they were interrupted or maybe they had done all they set out to do."

"How much do you think this will cost me?"

"Ten to fifteen thousand."

"Sweet Jesus, that much."

"Well, we really won't know until I get some estimates. You have insurance, don't you?"

"Sure, but after this claim I bet they'll drop me like a lead balloon."

"Maybe so, needless to say our sales prospect left in a big hurry when they saw the house."

"How long do you think it will be before the house is ready to show?"

"Three, four months."

"It can't be done any sooner?"

"That'll cost you extra I'm sure."

"Fine, I don't care anymore I just want to get this albatross out of my life. You do what you think will expedite this mess and give me a call with the estimates. Do I need to come down there or go to the police station?"

"No, I gave them your cell phone number. They'll give you a call. I sure do wish I had been calling you with good news instead of this."

The police called later that night. Richard arranged to meet with the investigator at a little dinner around the corner. Joe Turner, the investigator in charge, presented him with an array of color photographs of the damage.

"Quite a mess, isn't it?" Joe said.

"I'll say. You have any idea who did it?"

"I was hoping you had some ideas."

"Alice said she thought it was kids, gang graffiti." Richard seemed a bit puzzled by the question.

"That's what Officer Larsen thought too. He was first on the scene, but the M.O. is wrong. Plus they found a small boom box, the kind you can buy at any discount store."

"Well, that certainly sounds like kids."

"All except for one thing. When you pushed the play button, out came 'I'm going to love you forever, forever and ever Amen.' There's nothing before it, nothing after it. My wife says it's a Randy Travis song. Mean anything to you?"

"Yeah, it does. My ex-wife. I guess you could say it was our song."

"Having a few problems with the ex lately?"

"Did, thought it was in the past though. I guess I'm just not that lucky to have been rid of her that easily, just because we're divorced. I have restraining orders against her. She's not to come within two miles of me or Quinn."

"Quinn?"

"Our daughter."

"People violate restraining orders all the time. When they want to get to someone, they usually find away. Right now, we don't have any real physical evidence to bring her in on. I could haul her in for questioning, but that's about it. Do you have any pictures of her? No, probably not. That was a stupid question, how about any information that might be helpful?"

"I don't. Alice described a woman that could have been her. I'll have my lawyer give you a call. I'm sure he'd be able to get what ever you need. Can you give me your business card?" Richard asked the officer.

"Sure and if you notice anything unusual give me a call. Okay?"

"Don't worry I will. I won't take any chances, not when it comes to Quinn. Maybe it's time I changed jobs and we moved again."

Richard and Quinn were home watching 'Beauty and the Beast' for the thousandth time. The phone rang, Quinn ran to pick it up.

"Daddy, there's nobody there, just breath."

"Hang up the phone, honey."

Quinn dropped the phone on the receiver and ran back to couch and snuggled up to her father. The phone rang again. Quinn started to get up.

"You stay right here, young lady. I don't want you to miss a minute of your show. Daddy will get the phone."

Just like when Quinn answered the phone there was nothing there except the faint sound of someone breathing, then a click. He had his phone disconnected the next day and used his cell phone instead. The only problem with that was no modem. That meant he'd have to save his work on a CDrom then bring it into the office until he could arrange for cable DSL.

Quinn didn't mind going to the office with her dad. The women doted over her. They gave her candy and gum and let her touch the buttons to all the machines. Daddy's computer was off limits. Quinn sat on what was left of Sara's lap (she was due any day) banging away at the keyboard, while Richard talked with Adam. Adam was trying to convince him to renew his contract to no avail. Richard had made up his mind that he was going to do consulting work only and that was that. Adam didn't like it but he understood. He wished him well and promised to keep in touch.

He and Quinn practiced skipping on the way to the car. Quinn beat him to the car by a split second, just as she always did.

"Daddy, your car's all scratched."

Richard reached down to pick up Quinn; he held her close as he walked around his car. Scratched was an understatement, gouged was more like it. He checked inside the car before restraining Quinn in her seat, just in case. He decided to drive straight to the local police department, calling Joe Turner from his cell phone as he did. Joe said he'd meet him at the station. Something inside him told him to ask Richard what route he was taking. This happened to be a very good thing, because the next thing he knew his car was rammed from behind. Quinn screamed.

An old battleship of a car had nearly jolted his brand new Jetta off the road. Even though he could not tell who was driving, he knew it had to be Tanya. Before he could gain full control of his car, the gold monstrosity slammed him again. This time he reacted by speeding away, the old clunker not far behind. As he entered the more populated area of town, he was plagued with stop signs and signals. At every stop, he checked his rearview mirror. At an intersection near a park, Tanya appeared out of nowhere slamming once again into the rear of his car, pushing the car through the intersection and up over the curb into a lamppost.

Joe had just come up to the same intersection from a different direction in time to see Richard's disabled vehicle and Tanya backing up to take another go at him. He pushed the gas pedal to the floor and hit the old jalopy at the front driver side, spinning her around, away from the VW. He raced out of his car to restrain the driver from leaving. Her head was resting on the steering wheel. While she was out cold, he cuffed her to her steering wheel and removed the keys.

Richard and Quinn were lucky. The car was totaled but they came out with out a scratch, not a physical scratch that is. They still had to deal with the trauma of the ordeal. Of course, that was more Richard's cross to bear. Quinn thought they had just been in a bad accident. She was not aware her own mother just tried to kill them. Tanya was locked up and charged with aggravated assault.

After their visit to the hospital, to make sure they were all right, Richard and Quinn took a taxi home. This almost proved to be a mistake. Quinn was sound asleep in his arms when he opened the door to the town home. The place was trashed in the same manner as the house, only this time you could read the writing on the living room wall, "Forever and ever, Amen." He turned around, closed the door, and took Quinn to a motel. Joe was informed of the destruction.

Richard and Quinn moved into a small house just south of Buffalo that same week. Adam threw out all the trashed items in the townhouse and had movers packed up the rest. Alice arranged for the repairs and the sale of his second home.

***

The trial lasted six weeks, and in the end Tanya was pronounced guilty but insane. His lawyer assured him this was better than a straight conviction for aggravated assault. With a straight conviction, she could have been released early with good behavior. This way she would have to prove herself sane before she could be released. After what he saw in the courtroom, he thought that it would be a burden too large for her to overcome. With Tanya locked up he felt a sense of freedom. A heavy oppressing weight had been lifted from his life. Maybe now he could restore some normalcy to he and Quinn's life. He could go to work, she to school, and they could venture out to the grocery store and even the park with out fear that Tanya would show up. It seemed too good to be true.

Quinn's fifth birthday was just around the corner. Next year she would start kindergarten. With four hours a day of peace and quite, he could concentrate on expanding his consulting business. The royalties from his patents were starting to dwindle down; newer products with new patents were now on the market. The houses had sold but he barely broke even on those transactions. The small rental house in Hamburg New York, outside Buffalo suited their needs and his budget, but it was nothing to write home about. Home, he didn't have anyone left back home where he grew up. The automobile industry had all but died back in Detroit, his parents with it. Richard was an only child like Tanya. Now all he had left was his precious daughter. This was now home, and he was bound and determined to make a go of it. An outside contractor had advantages; one being it did not matter where he lived. Once he made a name for himself he could pick and choose where to live. He was on line checking his stock investments when there was a knock at the door. His stocks were plummeting. The DOW and the NASDAQ were spiraling down. Recession was feared to be right around the corner. He had a pit in his stomach watching his hopes for the future flush down the drain. His only hope, the market would come back eventually, before he lost everything. Distracted by his portfolio, he had forgotten about the knock on the door. The mailman knocked again, this time a little louder. Richard shut down the screen on his computer and signed for the letter.

The certified letter was nothing more than a plain white envelope, no return address. There was no letter or card inside. He tried to remember what the handwriting looked like on that green peace of paper he signed. Was it Tanya's? Was it typewritten? He couldn't remember. He ran back to the door to see if he could catch the mailman but he was gone. It had to be Tanya. How did she find them? He called Adam.

***

Adam had inherited a two-bedroom chalet in Cayuga Lake, south of Rochester, in upstate New York. Adam's wife didn't like the country;

she had a thing about bugs, rodents, and large bodies' water. They had visited it once with disastrous results and never went back. Adam offered it to Richard as a rent to own. Richard and Quinn fell in love with the place the first time they saw it. To Richard it seemed as though it had been custom designed just for him. Everything about it was perfect, including the location. Even though city born and bred, Richard found the countryside was home to him. He and Quinn had settled in with nominal adjustments.

Quinn was a likable and outgoing little girl; she attracted friends and playmates wherever she went. Considering her short trauma-filled little life, this was a remarkable talent on her part. It was good for Richard too. He would have all but holed up and become a recluse if it hadn't been for Quinn. Her activities forced him to interact with other people. In a small town friends were important.

***

Richard picked up his tea and drank it down. It had a bitter after taste. That's right, he forgot the honey. He took the picture of him and Tanya and threw it back into the box. Turning the page, he began reading his novel. It wasn't long before his eyelids drooped with sleep. Reading and baseball games on the TV always did this. He attempted to shake it off. He turned to the next page, the letters started to blur. He reached over for his reading glasses. The table contained his empty cup, the TV remote, and an ashtray with an old stogie, but no glasses. He stood, determined to find them. A sudden wave of dizziness fell over him. He sank back into his chair. He thought, maybe it was the flu. It had been going around. He reached for the remote and clicked the TV on. He felt a little better and his eyes were able to focus. Flipping through the stations, searching for anything tolerable to watch, he decided cable was worthless. Switching over to the local networks, he found a re-run of the 'Body Snatchers' and knew it almost by heart. Only one problem, it was filled with commercials and newsbreaks.

He was just about to flip to another station when a teaser clip for the upcoming news ran. Something the reporter said caught his attention. Three women had escaped the psychiatric ward of a minimum-security prison in upstate New York on Wednesday. Thoughts started swimming in his head and he was having a hard time sorting through them.

"Why haven't I heard about this? Right, Right, the cable wasn't switched on until Friday. Today is Sunday, why was this still big news? What if it was Tanya that escaped? Why didn't anyone call me? Cell phone doesn't work up here; phone just set up through the cable, no one has the number yet. That's alright. Tanya can't possibly know where we are. Damn it, what happened to the news?" Richard's mind swam with questions. He stared at the television, it took four maybe five agonizing commercials before the programming went back to his show. There was no more news on the escapees. He leaned forward with the remote in his hand. His head started to swim. Jumping from station to station, he found himself back at his movie. The next few minutes were agony. The room started to spin, his stomach churned. Then the news flash lit the screen. At this point, the best he could do was listen, for he could barely see.

"Last Wednesday we reported that three women had escaped a psychiatric ward wounding a guard and killing another. As of today, only Abby Long, pictured here, is still on the loose. Sondra Davies was apprehended, shortly after the escape, shoplifting in a nearby liquor store.

This morning the body of the third escapee was found; we are awaiting identification through dental records and notification of the next of kin. Her burnt body was retrieved from a vehicle, which was found at the bottom of a ravine in Short Hills Park a few miles outside Niagara Falls. The guard is reported as critical but stable; more news at the top of the hour. This is Lonnie Kurtz with CBC news."

Richard leaned back into his chair.

"Sweet Jesus, was she coming for us again?"

He wasn't sure but he thought he heard the teapot whistle. He turned his head in its direction. There was that sweet smell again. What was that smell? He knew it, yes he did. It was Tanya's little girl cologne. The one she said she used in high school. She used it to signal Richard it was okay to approach her. He thought it was kind of sick. Her father loved the same cologne. The stereo kicked on. The speakers resounded with "I'm going to love you forever, forever and ever, Amen."

"Oh my god," Richard thought, "That wasn't Tanya's body they found."

He stood, turning his body as best he could towards the stereo to see a haggard looking woman staring back at him. Her black hair looked as though it hadn't been washed in a year. Her clothes were filthy and hung on her body like a sack covering nothing but bones. It was obvious she was back on methamphetamines. Tanya turned down the volume on the stereo. She was so impressed with her own cunningness that she wanted to make sure Richard would hear her as she touted her accomplishments.

"It's amazing what can get done when you have a lover that works as a file clerk in the prison's medical office. Don't you think it was

74

pretty clever of me, Dick? I think you forgot how resourceful I could be; you taught me computers were the wave of the future. You were so easy to track down. I'm so disappointed in you, Dick."

Richard's legs buckled beneath him and he fell catawampus into the chair. Tanya's smile was one of devious delight.

"Feeling a little woozy my love?"

***

Richard awoke on top of Quinn's bed. He didn't know how long he had been out but he could tell it was night. Tanya must have turned on the light next to Quinn's bed. He never noticed what a weird glow the little lamp made in her room until just now. He thought he would have to replace that stupid Disney lamp later. Later? Richard did not even know if there was going to be a later. He tried to move only he was pinned in, strapped down somehow. He lifted his head to see what was restraining him. Tanya had sown him up in a silk sheet with fishing line. She had done a right good job of it too. There was barely any leeway for movement. As his eyes focused and his senses returned, pain racked his body. He felt a burning sensation in his groin area combined with a headache that would put a bear down.

Tanya was in the kitchen making coffee. She hated tea. Tea was so pretentious. Oh, but she was pleased with herself. She had blind-sided this vermin of a man, before he even knew what hit him. She had been planning this for more than a year. Every little detail had gone as planned, except for the stupid guards that got in her way.

While in the psych ward, she read article after article on how different women had taken revenge on their men. She was most fond of two articles in particular. One where the wife poured lye soap on her husbands genitals while he was in a drunken stupor of sleep. He woke up with the skin burned so badly they had to remove his testicles. Her other favorite was where the man's live-in lover drugged him up then sewed him up in canvas. She then took a baseball bat and smashed every major bone in his body. Neither man was going to ever cheat on his woman again. She hummed along with the stereo, still playing the same song, as she contemplated her final move.

Richard lay helpless, hopeless on the bed. Fear and pain coursed through his body. His heart beat a rhythm of panic. He tried to skirt himself to edge of the bed, checking the door for Tanya's return. He didn't know what he would do even if he did manage to roll off the bed. Then he noted a baseball bat leaning against the foot of the bed. His heart beat so fast he thought he would die of a heart attack first.

Tanya doctored her cup of coffee, and added a couple of cookies to the saucer and brought it into the living room. She set it down on the table that was next to Richard's chair replacing the teacup.

"This is my reward for later."

She took the empty teacup into the kitchen and washed it clean, wiped her hands dry then entered Quinn's room. She leaned up against the door jam. There was an eerie calm about her.

"Hello DICK my love. Did you miss me? I missed you."

"Tanya, please don't go through with this. Think how this will hurt little Quinn. I know how much you love her. You wouldn't want to hurt her this way, would you?"

"You sound so pathetic. You wouldn't want to hurt Quinn this way, would you? You slime, like you really care about what happens to Quinn." She laughs, "Like I really care what happens to Quinn. I swear, you'd think she came out of your womb instead of mine. No DICK, I care only about one thing and that's to see you suffer like I suffered and if you happen to die in the process. Oh well."

Tanya picked up the baseball bat and struck him in the groin. Richard screamed out, almost passing out from the pain.

"Hurts a little, don't it? I wanted to make sure you were awake for this part, a little pain before the grand finale to attune the senses."

Tanya lifted the baseball bat over her head, preparing to smash him with great delight. The one thing Tanya did not count on was when she slammed him in the groin, his body doubled over with such force that the sheet ripped at the knee. In pure desperation, he forced his knee through the tear and managed to pull his right leg free. As Tanya swung the bat, Richard used every ounce of energy he had to roll off the bed as the bat slammed down on the empty bed. He landed with a thud on his face, breaking his nose. Tanya screamed with anger. "You bastard." She raised the bat with even more venom cursing through her veins, preparing to take another swing at him.

Blood rushing down his face, Richard swung his free leg around to face his screaming demon. His foot caught Tanya at her ankles, knocking her against the wall. She fell onto the hard wood floor. Undaunted by this momentary set back, she struggled back to her feet. She raised the bat high over her head, and then paused. Her ghoulish face turned an ashen white. She gasped for air. It appeared Tanya's venture in drugs had at last resulted in what the doctors had been warning her for years. Her heart was giving out. Richard took advantage of her hesitation. He kicked at her again, causing her to topple over. Only this time she fell on top of him. She fell dead. The weight of her body crushed against him like that of a three hundred pound man. His arms were still tightly bound in the silk sheet so he struggled to pull his legs up to push her off. The pain of his crushed pelvis cursed through his body and his legs fell limp. All he could think of was he didn't want Quinn to see him like this.

***

Large gentle snowflakes fell. It was soothing to just sit and watch them fall like feathers to the ground. Quinn sat tailor-fashioned on the floor next to the Christmas tree, looking through the bountiful arrangement of packages.

"Daddy, can I open one now?"

"Sure hon just let daddy come over there first, so I can watch."

Richard wheeled his chair away from the living room window. The doctors said they thought he should be able to walk on his own in a year, after a few more surgeries. It was going to be a long haul to recovery.

Quinn picked out the largest package with bright red paper and squealed with delight.

"Daddy, can I open this one first?"

"Sure pumpkin."

He smiled as his little girl tore the paper off with no mercy.

"Oh, daddy. This is exactly what I prayed for."

She pulled out her very own lap top computer. One he had designed just for teaching kids. Quinn ran over and threw her arms around Richard's neck, and gave him a big kiss on the cheek.

"Thank you daddy. You're the best daddy in the whole world. I'm goin to love you forever and ever."

A chill ran down Richard's spine; to hear these words made him almost cry in anguish. He replied with as much calm and love his voice would allow him.

"You're welcome, Quinn. I love you too, with all my heart. I love you."

Quinn sat on the floor playing with her very own computer. Richard noticed the book he had found had been placed back on the table next to his easy chair. He wheeled over to the table and picked the book up. The picture of Tanya and him had been placed back in the book with the edges sticking out as a bookmark. He opened it to reveal the page where she had made her inscription, only now there was an addition to it. "Forever ends now." He placed the book in his lap and wheeled over to the fireplace, staring at the roaring flames. Then without a second thought he threw the book into the flames.

"You're right, forever has ended."

The Incident at Green Valley Lake

Labor Day weekend saw the last of the tourists for a few months. The secluded and little known community of Green Valley Lake resumed its diminutive 'full timer' population. School was back in session and while the Inland Valley still sweltered under a hundred plus temperatures, the mountains were showing the first signs of fall. Fire season was again a prevalent threat. The previous fall had proved to be devastating to the San Bernardino Mountains. Most of the summer had been tagged as a 'very high' fire hazard. Yet for three friends Travis, Alexandria and Brent the cool air spoke of the coming winter, snow, sledding, snow boarding, skiing and Christmas, the next main vacation time from the drudgery of school. It wasn't that school was so bad, it was just school. Travis was the only one of the three who seemed to really look forward to it. Brent didn't mind football season but Alexandria couldn't find a redeeming quality in any of it.

Travis had been home schooled until he outgrew the instruction his parents and local tutors were able to provide, and high school was already proving to be inadequate for his voracious appetite for knowledge. The advanced math and science classes were offering little challenge, and his parents were considering a private tutor from the university until he could enroll in the online classes offered by a university. Travis's goal was to be an astrophysicist, preferably for NASA. Anyone who knew Travis was sure he would not only obtain his goal but also exceed even his wildest dreams.

Alex was not like other girls her age. While her classmates were focused on their new clothes, fingernail polish, jewelry, and boys. Alex had little or no interest in any of it. She spent a lot of time with her father fishing and going on odd jobs in the area, mostly carpentry. She idolized her father and he adored her. Having no boys in the family lineage and her father's undying attention, Alex was predestined to be a tomboy. A tomboy she was and proud of it. As far as boys were concerned, they were merely fun to hang out with. They were certainly more fun and definitely more interesting than girls.

Brent was a guy's guy. Most of his football buddies could not understand why he would hang out with such a geek as Travis, but he liked Travis and considered him his best friend. He came home with many a black eye or fat lip defending Travis from bullies. It didn't matter to him. In fact he wore his battle wounds as badges of honor in the defense of the little guy, even if he was a geek. Brent and Travis met when they were just two years old and had been inseparable ever since.

Although Brent would never admit it to his buddies, he rather enjoyed the challenge of Travis's critical thinking. It was not unusual for Travis to pose a question or an idea while fishing out of Brent's father's canoe or while camping out in the backyard. He particularly liked the ongoing discussion on time travel. Ultimately, however, Travis came to the conclusion that mathematically, time travel was impossible.

Brent and Travis stood in front of the community center, across the street from the little post office waiting for the school bus to pick them up. They were talking and goofing around when a car pulled up. Alex exited the front passenger side and walked over to them. She signaled her mom to go on but the car did not budge.

"Mom, we'll be alright. There's three of us here, we'll be fine, go."

"No, I think I should stay. Just in case."

"Mom!" She said incredulously. "Look, Heather and her brother Andy are on their way down. It's okay!"

Alex's mother turned her head to the right to see the other children coming down the road. Andy was a big kid for his age and she felt comforted by his size and their numbers. "Alright, but I'll be here to pick you up directly after school. I'll give you boys a ride if you want, love you." She slowly pulled away, pausing as she took a turn in the road to take one last look.

"What was all that about?" Brent asked.

"She's just being over protective after this weekend, that's all."

"What happened this weekend?" Brent questioned.

"Yeah, I know. My mom wouldn't let me leave the house until Brent showed up. She even suggested I take my slingshot with me but I reminded her I would get expelled if I brought it to school. So, I put a bunch of rocks in my pocket and that seemed to make her feel better."

"What are you guys talking about? What happened this weekend?" Brent demanded.

"You didn't tell him?" Alex asked.

"No, I figured I'd let you do it since it happened at your house and your much better at story telling than I am. Plus, it gives me the willies to even think of it." Travis shivered.

"Alright, give. I can't take the suspense. Spill the beans Al before my brain explodes." Brent begged.

"Okay, okay! Saturday morning, Dad and I were sitting at the kitchen table sorting through the tackle box deciding what lures to put in the travel case. Dad also wanted to put new line on the reels, so we needed to get an early start. Mom and Callie were still asleep or at least we thought they were both asleep. Travis was cutting through the back like he always does when he comes over, when he realized he had just crossed the path of a small pack of coyotes, and this pack had adopted a stray rottweiler. We had heard them earlier that morning, but they sounded so far away. Travis said he stood very still and very quiet hoping they had not seen him, but they did. It was the rottweiler that turned and growled at Travis and then started toward him. Bennie started going crazy, barking at the door. Dad shushed him and then heard the growling and the coyotes yipping. I held on to Bennie while Dad grabbed his rifle from the rack and went to the back door just in time to see Callie run out. She had pushed a chair over in front of the door so she could reach the lock and out she went. Dad nearly broke his neck tripping over the chair to get out the door. He ran onto the back deck, grabbed Callie with his left hand, and cradled her under his arm like a football. When Callie went out the door it caught the attention of one of the coyotes. One started to stalk her, but when Dad flew open the door it stopped in its tracts. He yelled at it and stomped his feet and it scurried back a few feet but was not willing to leave altogether. That's when Dad noticed Travis and the rottweiler preparing to pounce him. Callie was kicking and screaming at the top of her lungs. I threw Bennie in the bathroom and I ran out behind my Dad. He yelled at me to get back into the house but I grabbed Callie under her arms and yanked. I screamed, "I've got her, Dad," then I ran with her inside the house and slammed the door. Mom came running down stairs. I don't think I had ever seen such terror in anyone's face before. She grabbed Callie from me and held her in her arms sobbing. I heard dad yell out, "Travis, whatever you do, don't move." Just then I heard the sharp crack of the rifle going off, then two more shots in a row, a pause, and then one more shot. The door flew open and Travis flew in and closed the door behind him. He was as white as a ghost. As soon as he caught his breath he said, "I'm sure glad your Dad is a good shot. He got three of them and he's chasing down the other two. Shit, I've never been so scared in my life. I thought I was a goner." He later apologized to my mom for swearing, but she says she never heard him say it. Mom was a basket case for the rest of the day. She wouldn't even come down stairs when animal control came over to take a report and cart the bodies away."

"Damn, I always miss all the excitement around here. Did your Dad get the other two?" Brent asked.

"No, Dad thinks he nicked one of them but they took off into the hills. Where were you this weekend? I called but no one answered."

"I told you didn't I? I had to go down to San Diego for my Grandparents fiftieth wedding anniversary. The only cool thing about it was we got to stay in some fancy hotel, eat out, and go swimming in a roof top pool."

"Oh yeah, right, for some reason I was thinking that was next weekend." Alex responded.

"The biggest bummer was we never did get to go fishing. Alex's mom refused to let any of us out of her sight, and my mom, well let's just say she's on the same page as Mrs. Andersen." Travis added.

"Not exactly on the same page. I don't think your mom is having a six-foot chain link fence placed all round your house, electrified!" Alex sneered.

"Ah, no way. It's gonna look like my grandparents' house. I hate it that all the city people have fences. At least most of them don't fence in the front yard. That sucks. Your front yard was one of the better ones to sled down in the winter. We could start there and sled all the way down to the church non-stop. Al, isn't there something your dad could say or do to make her change her mind. I mean he obviously got her to change her mind on having a rifle in the house." Brent asked.

"Mom said yes to the rifle after Bennie got dragged down the street by a coyote. If it hadn't been for old man Carpenter coming out with pots and pans clanging them together, Bennie would have been coyote food. Nope, mom put her foot down. It was one thing to have the family dog nearly ripped to shreds, but it's another when her baby's life was at stake. She said it was either a fence or a for sale sign. Dad didn't think she was serious until he over heard her talking to a realtor Sunday afternoon about finding a house down in Riverside, closer to Dad's work."

The bus pulled up, and the five of them went in and took their usual seats, Travis by the window because he got motion sickness and said it helped when he could keep his eyes on something in the distance. Brent sat next to Travis, just in case someone decided to pick on him and Alex sat at the isle seat. Heather and Andy were older than they and really had nothing to do with them. Plus their parents had money and they both had that air of "We're better than you. We have a big house, nice clothes, and all the latest gadgets and get to travel. You are just local yokels, plain folks, working stiffs, the common people, while we only live here because our parents wanted us to experience rural living like they had when they were growing up." They were snobs and made no bones about looking down their noses at underclassmen and the locals. Andy and Heather went to the back of the bus. Alex supposed that was so they could make rude remarks about everyone who got on from then on. They were always whispering and snickering. It made Alex's skin crawl.

Travis leaned over Brent so Alex could hear him speak.

"You guys aren't going to move are you? Cuz, if you did my mom would be next in line. I swear the only thing that has kept us there was you moving in. Until then we were the only full-timers on our street. It spooked mom something fierce, especially if Dad had to work late." Travis asked nervously.

"No, Dad said he was going to measure out how many feet of fencing he needed and would make a stop at the hardware store on the way home from work. He says he may have to work down the hill but he doesn't have to live there. Anyway, he says he would rather deal with a few coyotes any day than have me have to deal with gangs in the city schools." Alex informed them.

"Yeah, I know the kind of kids your Dad is talking about. We have to play some of the schools down the hill, only the smaller ones. They still have twice as many students as we do but there aren't many schools in our division. The guys all come off as 'wantabe gang bangers' and the girls are even worse. Most of them have never been fishing or seen a coyote, couldn't ride a horse, or identify a bear two out of three times, but they know how to corner you in the boys' room and beat the crap out of you without a teacher ever knowing, and it's the girls that lure you there in the first place." Brent's face and voice was full of anger.

"It sounds to me like you have first hand knowledge." Alex was more concerned than curious but it was a subject Brent quickly wished he hadn't brought up.

"Alex," Travis refused to call her Al like Brent did. He thought she was way to pretty too be an Al. "That's one story you don't want to hear."

"Why?"

"Cuz, knowing your temper, you'd figure out a way to take revenge on these creeps, and you would be the one to get hurt." Brent retorted.

"You act as if I could ever meet up with these 'creeps.'" Alex said perplexed.

"Al, you could if certain things fell into place, you could." Travis jumped in and immediately regretted it.

"Like what things and what did they do to you Brent?" Alex insisted.

The bus pulled into the school parking lot and stopped in its designated area. The doors opened up and kids started pushing their way forward. The threesome sat there until most of them had emptied out.

"Brent, I asked you what things had to fall into place and what did they do to you?" Alex insisted.

Travis knew this was the last thing Brent would be willing to talk about, especially to Alex, but he also knew once Alex got her teeth into something they would be hard pressed to get her to change the subject. The only thing Travis could think of was to pretend he was going to get sick. It would not have been the first time.

"Augh, (hack, hack) Brent come with me to the boys bathroom. I think I'm going to be sick."

"Sure thing buddy. Alex, please?" Brent pleaded.

There was something so incredibly pathetic in Brent's eyes that she took pity on him and stood up to let them by. For the rest of the day Travis and Brent avoided her. In fact, for the rest of the week Brent had his father drive him to school early and pick him up late. He told his Dad that he was involved in a special school project and after school they were having football practice. It was only a half-truth.

Travis came over to the Andersen house early Saturday morning. He needed to talk to Alex to see if he could put things right again. It had been a miserable week trying to avoid talking to her, for fear she would press him about Brent.

"Hi, Mr. Andersen, is Alex home?"

Mr. Andersen stopped using the posthole digger for a moment, pulled out a bottle of water from his pant pocket, and then took a swig before he spoke.

"Yeah, she's inside watching TV with Callie. Go right in. I think Karen is baking some blueberry muffins, you might be just in time."

"Thanks, Mr. Andersen."

"Bob, call me Bob son."

"I can't do that sir. My parents would kill me if they found out I called you by your first name."

"They're from the old school are they? Hey, you and Brent are coming over tonight for Alex's birthday party, aren't you?"

"I am, I don't know about Brent. I haven't talked to him yet." Travis squirmed a little, knowing the current situation.

"Well, it just wouldn't be the same without the two of you. I have something special planned for this birthday. Something my Alex has been wanting for sometime and after her brave actions last week I decided I would spare no expense."

"Well, you sure have my curiosity up. Oh, and Mr. Andersen, thank you again."

"And for the twelfth time, you're welcome. Go on, I can smell those muffins now. They're best when their hot."

Travis hesitated for a moment then blurted out a question that had been weighing on his mind since the last weekend.

"Mr. Andersen, I've been wondering about the rottweiler packing with the coyotes? Isn't it unusual that they would allow a regular dog into their pack? I was searching on the Internet and I didn't find anything on the coyote packs taking in stray dogs."

"Some people call then Coydogs when they cross breed. They are supposedly rare but much more dangerous because 'regular dogs' as you put it, are not afraid of men like the coyotes. They are much more aggressive and so are their offspring. I wouldn't be surprised if the alpha female hadn't lost her mate to that rottweiler, and he became the alpha male in the pack. I also wouldn't be surprised if she has his pups this spring. Unfortunately, she was one of the two that got away. We have a real problem up here with people dumping dogs they no longer want. Somehow, people seem to think it is more humane to let them go out in the wild than take them down to the humane society. I guess they feel they have a better chance of survival. The larger dogs do, but when they mate with the coyotes they produce larger, more aggressive pups. I've turned over around five strays in the last two years. This last June I found a German Shepard pup tied up to a tree next to a water run off pipe with a bag of dry food down in Crab Flats. She was such a sweet little thing. I tried to talk Karen into keeping her but she would have none of it. She was not about to housebreak a dog and a child at the same time. I guess I don't blame her. Anyway, a pup has a much better chance getting adopted, than an older dog. I just don't understand people sometimes, especially when it comes to these rottweilers. I think they dump them because they were too aggressive in the first place, and probably threatened their own family or neighbors. Then they bring them up here and cause even a bigger problem. I'm just thankful that no one got hurt."

"Me too! Thanks Mr. Andersen. I'll look up coydogs on the internet when I get home."

Karen opened the front door and yelled out.

"Breakfast is ready. Come in and eat, before it gets cold." Then as quickly as she appeared, she was gone.

Travis and Alex ate at the coffee table in front of the television while her parents and Callie ate at the dinning room table. Travis had already eaten at home and took a muffin and some milk to be polite. He picked at his muffin and pretended to be interested in the silly cartoon playing on the screen. All the while, he was trying to think up a diplomatic way to talk to Alex about Brent while they were alone. Ultimately, he could not think of anything clever so he just blurted out.

"Alex, Brent called his dad to pick him up after school just so he didn't have to talk to you on the bus. I can't stand all this distance between us. I want things to go back to the way we were."

"Me too…" Alex said and Travis started to interrupt but she cut him short. "Before you go on I want you to know I will never, ever, ever bring it up again. Do you hear me? Not ever, if Brent wants to talk about it then fine. You let him know that, okay?"

"I already told him that's what you would probably say but…"

"But what?"

"He said he wanted to hear it from you."

"Fine, then I will call him right now."

"Alex do you think that's a good idea? Things are kind of raw right now."

"Well, it's not going to get any better if nothing is said or done. Dad always says, "The longer you let things fester, the worse they get." Alex leaned back on the table next to the couch and took the phone out of the receiver and dialed Brent. "Hi Brent? I just want you to know that I will never, ever ask you anything about…you know what…ever again.

Okay? Now my mom is having a barbeque, hamburger and hotdogs, tonight for my birthday, and I want you to come…of course we will have cake and ice cream…chocolate cake, chocolate chip cookie dough ice-cream all smothered in my mom's home made hot fudge…Yeah, I thought that would get your attention…at six…good. See ya later." She returned the phone to its base and gave Travis an 'I told you so look'. "There, it's done. He'll be here at six."

"You know it will be a little awkward at first."

"Maybe at first but if we just act normal things will be fine, you'll see."

By the time the guests were in the midst of devouring their meal, with Brent on his third helping and Travis on his second, the threesome had settled right back into their old routine. It was just as though nothing had happened, just as Alex had predicted. The party was being held on the back deck. Bob threw several logs in the outside fireplace to help stave off the chill in the air. Karen had strung Japanese lanterns and streamers to add to the festive atmosphere. About ten people had shown up for the occasion. Everyone seemed be talking at once but one conversation caught most everyone's attention. One of the adults brought up something they had heard on a late night radio talk show and Travis could not wait to insert his perspective.

"No, I'm serious. He said that the government was covering up the fact that we are visited almost daily by aliens." Alex's Aunt Sandy retorted.

"Well, he is absolutely correct. When it comes to California, we are besieged daily with illegal aliens and if we don't watch it, it will bankrupt this state. Not to mention that one of these days, if it hasn't already happened, terrorist will slip through and cause us a world of hurt." Bob said.

"No, I'm not talking about that kind of alien." Sandy snapped.

"I know you're not Sandy. It's just the concept of the other is so ridiculous that I find it best left to the science fiction writers." Bob snapped back in a most sarcastic tone.

"That's only because the government covers everything up and then puts out disinformation to make it seem ridiculous," Aunt Sandy said justifying her belief.

"The government with all its power and might could not cover up a blue stained dress, the president's affair with an intern, or keep all those pictures of Abu Ghraib out of the media's hands. Yet, you want me to believe 'the government' is competent enough to cover up something as big as evidence of aliens visiting from another world. Come on woman, live in the real world," Bob sniped, replete with more sarcasm.

Sitting beside Bob, Karen nudged him with her left elbow. "Bob, be nice now. There are a lot of people who believe this stuff. Otherwise these talk shows wouldn't have the following they have."

"Karen, I am being nice. I didn't call her any names. Although I could think of a few that would fit just fine and just because a few thousand kooks listen to this stuff doesn't mean it has a lick of truth to it," Bob retorted.

"So what, now you're calling me a kook?" Sandy took great offense to the suggestion.

"Well, if the shoe…" Bob almost blurted it out but Travis decided it was a fine time to interject.

"How about just misinformed or ill-informed?" His remark took Sandy by surprise. She glared at him incredulously. Those who knew Travis merely sat back and grinned. "First it's important to deal with what is scientifically known. We know the earth rotates on its own axis and then rotates around the sun as do the rest of the known planets. Our whole galaxy travels at an incredible rate. From all the studies I have read, there aren't many scientists that believe there is another planet, moon or star in **our** galaxy that could have evolved higher life forms. So, that leaves us to check out the next closest galaxy. Do you have any idea how far away that is from us?"

"No, of course not." Sandy said indignantly.

"It's one point five million light years away. That may not sound very far, until you realize that light travels at 386,000 miles per second, not a minute, per second. Our best efforts in a jet-powered aircraft is the SR-71 Blackbird which has the official record of about Mach 3.3. This is 3.3 times the speed of sound, which is around 761 miles per hour, which is not quite 42 miles per second. The Apollo 10 capsule upon re-entry into the earth's atmosphere managed to obtain speeds up to 24,790 miles per hour. Divide that by 60 seconds and it was only going 413.17 miles a second. That is a far cry from traveling at the speed of light and at the speed of light it would take generations to get there from here. So, even if we could increase our ability to travel at say one hundred and fifty thousand miles an hour, that's only two thousand five hundred miles per second. That would mean it would take us around eleven thousand years to get there. One, do you think anyone here would care much less remember we sent them, and two since every thing is in a constant motion, would they ever be able to find their way back to tell anyone?

Not to mention the amount of fuel it would take. So you see, it is fun to speculate but not scientifically feasible." Travis was quite please with himself in breaking down the information in what he considered easily understood terms. The look on Sandy's face said otherwise.

"Well, that was a whole lot of numbers young man. Obviously you're very good at math, but I heard they can defeat all that traveling problem with worm holes and bending space, stuff like that."

"Theories and speculation; they had to try and come up with something once they realized it couldn't be done."

"How about time travel, they must be working on that."

When Sandy mentioned time travel, Karen, Bob, Brent and Alex all started to laugh and in unison said, "Mathematically impossible!"

"What, what is this a conspiracy? How is it mathematically impossible?" Sandy said aghast.

"I think we have had enough astrophysics for one day. I say it's time for cake, ice-cream, and presents for my birthday girl." Bob piped in and agreements were heard from all around.

"It's getting a little nippy out here. How about we all go inside?" Karen suggested.

They all gathered inside, sang happy birthday, and gave Alex her gifts. There was the usual stuff, clothes for school, music CDs, video games, and a particularly ugly dress from her Aunt Sandy. Aunt Sandy beamed when she opened it.

"It never hurts to have a few girly things in the closet. You never know when you might get asked to a dance or something."

Alex looked up at her mother with pleading eyes. Karen gave her a half smile that told her, "it's alright we will take it back to the store right away for something, anything else. Now tell Aunt Sandy, thank you."

"Thank you Aunt Sandy, it was…very thoughtful of you."

Brent and Travis snickered. They knew there was no way on earth she would be caught dead in that thing. Bob decided there had been enough taunting of Sandy for one night and handed Alex a gift from him.

"Hey pumpkin, we can't forget my gift to my special girl." He handed her what was obviously a book wrapped in brown paper. "I wrapped it myself."

"I see that. Oh goody; another book."

"Not just any book, a very special book."

Alex ripped off the paper-bag wrapping paper to find a book on fly-fishing, casting, and lures. It even had an instructional CD. The instructions were for making various types of fly lures.

"Wow, this is really neat Dad but I don't have a fly pole."

"Oh, you don't? I could have sworn you did. Maybe you need to look under the table."

"Under the table? Dad…?" She leaned a little side ways and peeked under the table to see everyone's feet. "Dad, are you playing a joke…" Brent and Travis also slid their heads under the table to see what Mr. Andersen was talking about. Brent came back up and grinned, "Look underneath the table." He said most emphatically. Both their heads and shoulders disappeared from topside. Brent pointed to something taped to the underside of the table. All of a sudden, everyone heard an excited squeal from Alex. Bob's face lit up with a Cheshire cat grin.

"Oh daddy, it's what I've always wanted."

"Well, bring it up here so we can all see this special gift." Sandy demanded.

"I can't get the tape off, I'm afraid I'll break it."

Travis scooted under the table and gently removed the tape and handed Alex her new fly pole. She brought it up and immediately put it together then displayed it like a trophy.

"Oh Bob really, another fishing pole? This is your daughter not a son. It's about time you treated her so." Sandy said, interjecting her own personal opinion on the whole subject.

There was one place Karen did not allow her sister to tread and that was on Bob's love for his daughters or her. He was a good father and a wonderful husband. In fact, there were times she felt sort of sorry for the man, having to deal with all these females around him all the time. She knew, as the girls became hormone raging teenagers, his life was going to be full of misery. Sandy didn't have any children, by choice, and Karen was not about to allow her to belittle the moment. "Sandy, I wouldn't go there if I were you."

"What, I'm just saying he needs to…"

"Sandy, you have a long drive ahead of you. It's getting late, I think it is time we all say our goodbyes and call it a night." Karen said adamantly.

"Are you dismissing me?" Sandy could hardly believe her ears.

"Oh, I believe I am dismissing everyone, including you." Karen bit her tongue.

"I can't believe you are doing this to your own sister. I…" Sandy's husband John, who rarely spoke during these get-togethers, stood and grabbed Sandy's jacket off the back of the chair.

"Come on woman, don't get your panties all in a bunch. It's time to go before you manage to fit your other foot in your mouth."

"Foot in my mouth, John, what are you talking about?"

"The fact that you don't know frightens me. Now say goodnight, you know how much I hate driving down this mountain at night." He turned his attention to Alex, "That's one mighty nice fly pole. I hope you catch your quota every time you use it." Then he looked over to Karen, "Thank you. The food and festivities were fine, as usual. Oh, and young Travis, I did enjoy your little dissertation. I found it quite informative." He smiled and winked.

After everyone left, Alex and her Dad put the line on the fly pole. Bob put a lightweight sinker on the end so Alex could practice casting off the back porch. She quickly gave up because her back swing continually caught the string of lanterns. Travis's mom, still leery of coyotes, drove down to pick him and Brent up because she did not want them walking home in the dark. As Travis was leaving he turned to Bob and asked, "What does Alex's Uncle John do?"

"He's retired from the Air force. I believe he was one of the few who got to fly one of those Blackbirds you were talking about."

"No way, man I would love to talk to him about those planes."

"That might be one of those topics you just might be able to get him to talk about. Particularly to you, you might actually understand."

"Unlike his wife."

"Yes, unlike his wife. I think he gave up a long time ago trying to explain complex things to her. She's always been off into her own little world. As usual, the family get-together proved interesting and challenging but not necessarily desirable. As my dad always said, 'You can choose your wife but not your in-laws, those you just grin and bare.'

"Maybe, I'm lucky all my relatives live on the east coast." Travis's mom honked the horn. "I've got to go…hey, come on Brent, my mom is here…Thanks for everything Mr. Andersen. Fishing tomorrow?"

"You bet ya. Ready by seven."

"You bet ya." Travis said as he ran down to the car. Brent mirrored the same as he squeezed by. Bob smiled as the boys left and he turned to see Alex sitting on the sofa, one hand on her new pole. All in all it had been a good day, a very good day.

Alex was up long before the rest of the household. She wanted to sort through her father's tackle box to find just the right lures for the day. Only she had two problems; mid to late October brought frigid mornings, too cold to do much of anything other than cuddle up in a blanket on the couch or start a fire. She chose to sit by a roaring fire where she could pick and choose her lures on the coffee table. Her father had taught her the proper way of starting a fire in the fireplace, and she was quite comfortable handling the task. Her second problem was what lures to choose. Her book talked of dry lures and wet lures, caddis dries, mayflies or nymphs. She quickly realized she had a lot more to learn than just how to properly cast the line. Alex always enjoyed fishing with her dad. In fact, she didn't much care what they did as long as it was with her dad. Two years previously he had taken her to an outdoor expo in Pomona, and there she met her first woman fly-fisher champion. Her name was Diana, and she was tall, beautiful, and graceful, and not a girly girl. Ever since that day, Alex wanted nothing more than to be just like her. Today would be her first day towards that goal.

Travis spent the night at Brent's and they stayed up way too late, playing video games, something Travis's mom frowned on. Travis loved the mindless games of chase them down and shoot 'em-up', and Brent could not wait for Travis's next science updates. Things like the Hubble space telescope taking pictures of the Kepler supernova, which occurred four hundred years ago, and how it was possible to see the remnants of something that happened so long ago. They talked long into the night. So, when the alarm went off at six, Travis pleaded for ten more minutes of sleep but as soon as he rolled over he realized his bladder was not about to let that happen. He dragged himself out of bed to relieve himself and when he came back he found Brent tying the laces to his shoes ready to go.

"Have you ever had a feeling that something extraordinary was going to happen?" Brent asked.

"All the time."

"I don't mean just in the realm of science…but maybe. I mean I have this feeling that something big, spectacular, frightening and awesome is going to happen."

"What, we will see some of Aunt Sandy's shadow people?"

"Maybe, but I was more thinking on the lines of that alien creature known as King Albert wiggling on the end of one of our lines."

They both giggled.

It was highly debated among avid fishermen if King Albert even existed, and then it depended on whom you talked to whether or not King Albert was a rainbow trout, bass, or a twenty-pound catfish. It really didn't matter much to the kids, but rumors, such as King Albert, were great fodder for attracting fishermen to the lake.

The four of them took up their usual spot across the lake, away from the main road into town. The boys started off fishing from the bank but soon found they were being whipped by Alex's fly line. In her frustration she would yell at them, "You're in my way," or "Get out of my way!" She rebuffed any assistance they had to offer so they unchained Brent's dad's canoe and rowed out a distance from shore. Here they found the peace and quiet they had come for. Bob allowed Alex her pig-headiness to learn on her own, helping her only when she asked for it. For the better part of the day that help consisted of retrieving her line and hook out of a tree or untangling her line. Even when she put on her mother's waders, which where much too large, and stood in the shallow water, she still tried to strong-arm the cast. It was not until her arm tired that she realized that a soft even swing with the release just above her head was what she needed to obtain any distance with the line.

Around four o'clock, Bob checked his watch and decided it was time to call in the boys. That way they would still have some day light for the walk home. Brent and Travis rowed in and tied up the canoe. They proudly displayed the fish they had caught, two each.

"Hey, Mr. Andersen how did you do? We caught a total of four. No King Albert though, so much for Brent's premonition," Travis quipped.

It was always a competition between them for who could catch the most fish, and this time Travis could not help teasing Brent on his non-existent premonition. Bob pulled his stringer, which held three beauties, out of the lake. Alex blanked, but she thought she was getting the hang of how to cast her line.

"Look guys, it takes a few times but I can get it pretty far out there now. Dad, can we stay just a little bit longer? It's almost time for the fish to swirl."

"Sorry pumpkin. I promised your mom I'd have you home well before dinner so you would have time to bathe. You know how much she hates the smell of fish and fish bait."

"Just a couple more casts, please?"

"Okay, three more casts." Bob acquiesced.

"You're the best dad."

On her third cast, Alex turned her head back to see where her father was standing to make sure she did not snag him. She noticed an object coming over the trees, a few hundred feet up. It seemed to be coming straight at them.

"Dad, look!"

All four of them had their eyes fixed on the object in the sky. There were a few fishermen still scattered around the shoreline that day but most were unaware of the approaching object. There was no sound coming from it, nor was there any wind, at least not at first. What was really strange was they all had this desire to run out of the path of the impending doom but it seemed as though everything, including themselves, was moving in slow motion. It was almost as if time had stood still. Then they watched as a ball of fiery light passed overhead and continued to follow the curvature of the land. It was moments later that they heard and felt its passing. The sound was not a roar but a whizzing noise, and the air sort of just swooshed past them. There was no real air turbulence. Then just a short distance away, down towards Crab Flats Road, there was an explosion. They could see the glow from it where they stood. The light had an eerie blue-green glow to it that lasted for only a moment, and then it was gone. A light that would be more associated with something electrical as when the electricity arcs from one of the substations. It was within minutes the fire department dispatched engines to contain the fire they thought the object had caused. Shortly after the fire engines roared away, two military jets sped by at a very low altitude. The noise was deafening and when the sonic boom hit, the air shook. They could hear glass breaking all around and car alarms going off everywhere. Bob grabbed his pole and tackle box then started up the street at a quick pace.

"Come on kids, we need to get back to the house. I need to start watering down the roof of the house and you need to let your parents know to do the same. Worse case scenario, if the fire gets out of control, we might need to evacuate the mountain, again."

"What do you think that was, Mr. Andersen?" Brent asked.

"It was probably a meteor."

"Then why were the jets chasing it?" Travis found it odd that the military would chase a meteor.

"Maybe they had been tracking it on radar and wanted to know where it hit. If it hit in a populated area they would have to call in emergency services."

"What if it was a terrorist's missile and it just went by so fast we couldn't tell what it was?" Brent theorized.

"Hmmh, I never even considered that. If it was a missile, I guess we are lucky it didn't detonate properly." Bob said.

"What if it was chemical or biological? They are always talking about that." Travis added to Brent's theory.

"Come on you guys, you're scaring me. Oh man, look at that house. All the windows are shattered…and that house too. Mom and Callie must be scared half to death. Wonder if our windows busted?" Alex said breathlessly.

They turned down their street. All of them getting hot, sweaty, and a little out of breathe with the pace they were walking.

"I have plenty of plywood if they did but right now I am more concerned about fire." Bob responded.

As they approached the Andersen house, Alex could see her mom standing on the front porch, holding a crying Callie. She called out to Bob, "What's happened? I heard a loud crack and the sliding glass doors shattered. I'm so glad we were in the kitchen. Did I hear fire trucks?"

Bob was too winded to respond. Brent and Travis continued up the road, and then Travis turned around and yelled, "Alex, you want to give your fly-pole another try tomorrow? Providing we don't have to evacuate the mountain, that is."

"Yeah, see you about eight? I want to sleep in."

"Eight? You can't do that, you have school tomorrow." Her father barked.

"No, we don't. There's a teachers conference or something."

"Oh, that's right…listen." Bob leaned his ear towards the fire-station as it sounded an all-clear siren. "They must have been able to put the fire out really quick. Hm, they've barely had enough time to drive all the way down much less put out a fire, very odd." Bob said as he looked at his wristwatch.

Bob and Karen, like most of the full-timers, spent most of the evening cleaning up broken glass and doing their best to board up windows to prevent the night's cold from entering their homes. Travis and Brent went to their respective homes and helped do the same. Sometime around ten that night Travis decided to go on line and do a search on the Internet. What he found captivated and astounded him. Travis decided to see if Alex and Brent were online and IM'd them.

"sightings as far away as Brentwater England
in the Rendlesham Forest, Wales, NY, Ohio, Iowa,
New Mexico, Nevada and more. Airline pilots
overseas and across the states report sightings.
Maybe Brent did have a premonition. Explains
the military Jets. How bout a hike down to Crab Flats?"

Brent responded with a :) but Alex was not so sure and hesitated. Brent typed out, "Al, r u there?"

"Yeah, thinking!"

"Al!!!!!!!!!!!!!!!!!!!!"

"K but we go bak way…past the ol mining shaft
…away from the off roaders…k…meet at holcomb
@ 8:30"

It was decided; the three of them would venture down to see if they could find where the explosion had occurred.

Whatever fears the locals had regarding the fire was abated when it started to rain sometime during the night. When Alex woke up she was disappointed to see the rain. Yet, a part of her was glad. Even though she had agreed to trek down to Crab Flats, she was most uncomfortable with the prospect. Some things were just best left for the adults to explore and handle. The living room was darker than usual due to the plywood hammered over the sliding glass doors but the window above it was still intact and it allowed in some light. Here she could see the steady drizzle of rainfall. She loved to watch the rain from inside. Especially, when there was a roaring fire in the fireplace. The phone rang and took her out of her peaceful trance.

"Hello."

"Hi, this is Travis. I thought the rain was going to ruin our plans today but Brent has an idea."

Alex listened for a while then hung up the phone. She mulled over the plan, debating on whether or not to go through with it. Then she heard the words come from her mouth.

"Mom, I'm going over to Brent's to play video games with him and Travis."

Karen came out of the kitchen, wiping her hands on a dishtowel.

"Oh no you don't young lady. Brent's mom works and that means there will be no one there to supervise you."

"Mom, I'm old enough to watch other peoples' kids and you leave me here alone with Callie all the time. Come on, I'm twelve years old and Brent is thirteen. Obviously, his mom and dad think he's old enough to stay home alone."

"But I'm sure they didn't give permission for him to have a bunch of kids over and destroy the place. No, they can come over here."

"Fine…I'll call them and tell them to come over here and mess our place up. Hope you have plenty of food for lunch and snacks. You know how they like to eat." Alex had gotten pretty good at the reverse psychology. Her mother was starting to catch on to her but this time the thought of cooking and cleaning up after two boys, with no recourse of sending them outside to play if they got too rambunctious, was more than she could deal with on this rainy morning.

"Alright, alright, you can go but I don't want you kids going outside."

"Mom it stopped raining, see."

"Well, it's cold and wet still."

"I have my hooded jacket and my boots on. I love to take a walk right after it rains. Everything smells so fresh. I'll be fine."

"But absolutely no wandering anywhere near Crab Flats. Is that understood?"

Alex held her hand behind her back and crossed her fingers, "Understood."

"It's the strangest thing though, I have been watching the news all morning and there has barely been any mention at all about what happened yesterday. Just one little blip about some pilots out of Twenty-nine Palms who were grounded for flying too low and causing windows to break in some of the mountain communities. Don't you think that's strange?"

"Very!"

"Well, there's a neighborhood watch meeting tonight. Maybe someone there will be able to shed some light."

Alex knew if she didn't break for the door soon, her mom would continue talking. Her mom loved to talk. Alex thought maybe it was because she only had Callie to talk to all day. So she did not respond to her mother's last remark and went to the back door.

"Bye mom."

"I'll be calling to check up on you, you know?"

Alex looked back at her mom before she closed the door and said, "I know!" then quietly, too low for her mother to hear, "I love you too."

Brent and Travis had put together three day-packs by the time Alex arrived. They were replete with water bladders, chips, cookies, trail mix, and some beef jerky. They were anxious to get going as soon as she walked in the door.

"Here Al, this one is for you. I can't wait to get down there and see what we can find."

"Brent, my mom said she was going to call and check up on us. I think we should wait an hour before we go. That way maybe the fog will lift a little bit too."

"Hey no problem Al, we have that all covered. Travis here has a little hand held recorder and he recorded us playing a video game, about ten minutes worth. He also programmed my mom's cell phone, she forgot it this morning, to pick up any calls that comes to the house phone."

"Okay, that covers that aspect but what about getting lost in the fog? It's over three miles to the camp ground."

108

"Not to worry, ol'worrisome Al. We have that covered too. I took Dad's GPS tracker out of his backpack, put new batteries in and have spares in my pack, and Travis is programming the route right now. Dad always keeps the local maps in it. We hike down to Deep Creek all the time to fish. Plus, we are going to bring Hugo with us. He probably knows the trail better than that GPS. So you see, we are all set to go."

Travis came over and handed the GPS to Brent.

"Do you know how to work this thing?"

"Not really, my Dad always takes care of it. He's shown me a couple of times but I always get mixed up which buttons do what."

"Do you mind if I keep it with me?"

"Heck no! Just don't loose it. My dad would kill me."

Travis put his jacket on, zipped it up, flipped up the hood, slipped the tie through a small loop on the GPS, and then tied both strings to the hood together. This allowed the GPS unit to rest about midway down his chest, pulling the hood taught against his head.

"There, where I go it goes."

"Geez, you're such a geek. Come on let's go. I'll go get Hugo's leash."

Hugo was the family dog, although he seemed to favor Brent with affection and his Dad with obedience. Being an Australian cattle dog, he was not the kind of breed that would wander off. In fact, Hugo tended to keep everyone together in a nice little pack. This was kind of annoying to Alex because one of the ways he herded was to nip at your hands and feet. It didn't hurt. It just annoyed her. She did not like dog slobber on her hands.

They walked for about an hour before they took their first break. The path was a little slippery due to the rain and they had not traveled very far. All of them had slipped and fallen a few times and were getting pretty dirty and wet. Alex found a log to sit on.

"Oh great! Now my butt is wet too. I don't care what anyone says, we're taking the road back."

"Hey, you're the one that insisted we take the back way." Brent barked back.

"I know, but now that we stopped, I'm getting cold."

Hugo growled and then gave out two deep-throated oofs, not barks, oofs. Brent tugged on his leash.

"Shh, Hugo. What do you hear? Huh boy?"

Travis looked at the GPS and played with it a bit, then realized they were maybe a hundred yards from the road.

"The road is right over there. I can't see it but I think I hear a car coming down the road. Hey, come over here and look. I can see the headlights of one, two, three…man there's a whole bunch of trucks coming down this road."

Brent and Alex went over to where Travis was standing, Brent with a tight reign on Hugo. They could see the headlights and a faint outline of the vehicles but not much more.

"Man, I'm going to get into so much trouble if I get caught." Alex whined.

"Alex we're all going to get in trouble if we get caught. We all got the same lecture…Brent do you have those binoculars handy?"

"Yeah sure, hold on let me get them out of my backpack."

Brent ripped off the backpack and unzipped the outside pocket, then threw them to Travis. Travis had a hard time focusing them due to the fog obscuring his vision.

"Hold on a second…there I got it. Holy cow, those are military trucks. This must be really important for the military to come all the way up here."

"Are they wearing any kind of protective gear?" Brent asked.

"Man…I can barely see the trucks much less anyone in them."

"Here, you hold the dog. Let me take a look." Brent peered through the binoculars. "Man, there sure are a lot of 'em. Oh crap, that means they are going to get down there before we do. Are there any short cuts on that thing?"

"Hold on, let me see. Well, if we go straight that way but that's difficult to say. It looks like there are some hills but the road they are taking curves out then comes back in. They have to go pretty slow because of all the rain and the mud. So, maybe we could beat them there." Travis deduced.

"Oh great, so now we are going to run up and down muddy hills. One of is bound to get hurt" Alex whined again.

"Al, we've come this far. We only have maybe an hour and a half, maybe two more to hike. Do you want to give up now? We may never find out what happened if we turn back now." Brent coaxed.

"We may never find out what happened if we go on. I don't know who's doing it, but they are already covering up the sighting of the object, the explosion, and they are saying the jets were out on a routine flight and the pilots veered off course and they were flying too low, hot dogging it, one reporter said. My mom said there was barely any news about it. Except for all the broken windows they didn't make any big deal about it. And personally, I didn't think the explosion was at Crab Flats. Crab Flats is still way that way and from what I recall "it" was headed more towards Lake Arrowhead, towards Deep Creek Campground." Alex countered.

"Ah ha, she's right. I remember now. Those guys are going the wrong way. Not only that, I don't care what kind of off road vehicle they have, it won't get them there. Travis, re-map that thing with a heading towards Deep Creek." Brent could barely contain his excitement.

"I don't know. That's some pretty rugged terrain." Travis took his turn to whine.

"No it's not, not all of it anyway. Travis, picture it in your mind and try and fix it on the GPS. Come on Bud, you can do it. I know you can." Brent insisted.

"Yeah, it was close, really close. Why does everyone remember it being far away and in the other direction?" Alex asked as she watched Travis fiddled with the GPS.

"I don't know Al but we did too." Brent pondered.

"Think about it, if the explosion had been at Crab Flats we probably would not have been able to see it, at least not much of it unless it was really big. I mean it was big, but not that big." Travis added as he adjusted their headings. "I remember looking over at you and your father as that thing came towards us. It seemed the closer it got the slower everyone moved. I don't even remember it going over or past us, just seeing the explosion. There I've got it. Take a look and see if you all agree." Travis said after he was satisfied with the new co-ordinates.

"Okay…what am I looking at?" Alex asked. "Where's the lake in relationship to where we are going?"

Travis pressed on a button that panned out to include the lake area.

"Here is that better?"

Alex and Brent looked down at the view screen then up at Travis.

"That's exactly it. How far is that from where we are now?" She asked.

"It's just over that hill there and down the ravine. It's real close to where we built that tree house. Remember Brent?"

"Yeah, that was a fun summer but a lousy tree house and your right it's really close. Maybe another thirty-minute walk but we will have to wait until all these trucks have passed by. It's funny; we were closer to it when we started than we are now."

They picked up their packs and slung them over their shoulders. Just as they did the cell phone rang. Startled they jumped, and then they stood frozen in a temporary quandary as what to do. Brent took the phone out of his pocket and handed it to Alex.

"Here you answer it. Travis, take out the recorder out and play back the tape. Hurry up now before it goes to my mom's voice mail."

"Hello…Hi mom… (Travis held the recorder up in the air) nothing just playing games. I don't know, some racing game…yeah, its okay…no we've been eating all morning…no not just junk, good stuff too…. you know fruit and stuff…sure, I'll be home before its dark…promise…love you too, bye." She pressed the end button. "I'll be grounded for the rest of my life if she finds out we came out here."

"Al, you promised you wouldn't go to Crab Flats, and were not"

"I don't think she'll see it that way. I did just lie to her."

"Al, make up your mind now…cuz the trucks are going and we need to go before more come down the road. Are you with us?" Brent asked.

She looked over at Travis and Brent, whose faces beamed with the excitement of the adventure. Over the past couple of years, the three of them had been inseparable. The thought of them going off without her on this grand adventure was more than she could bear.

"Of course I am going with you. I wouldn't miss this for anything."

As the morning sun began to burn the fog away it became easier to find their way. The closer they came to the old tree house they more excited they became. Finding what everyone else was looking for and the anticipation of discovering it, made them feel giddy, warm and light.

At first it was barely noticeable but as the tree house came into view Brent remarked at how little effort it took to walk.

"Stand still for a moment Brent…look down at your feet. They aren't touching the ground. That's impossible…unless whatever is here is causing a gravity field." Travis deduced.

"Wouldn't that make me heavier? I feel as light as a feather." Brent said.

"Maybe it's a reverse gravity field," Travis said trying to figure out what was going on. Everything he had learned in his short life told him that what he concluded could not be possible. It just wasn't mathematically possible.

"I feel it too, don't you Travis?" Alex asked.

"No." He lied. "But I think I'll hang on to the trees as I walk just in case. Don't go too far ahead of me. I want to take pictures of all of this."

The area where Brent and Travis had built their tree house was at the edge of a flat area of the forest before a very steep ravine. It had a spectacular view of the valley below. As the tree house, what was left of it, came into view, Hugo whined and refused to go forward. This was most unusual for him, for he tend to run ahead a few feet. Brent tried to coax him along to no avail.

"Fine then, you just stay there." Brent said in exasperation.

Travis continued to walk making sure he never let go of a tree, no matter how small. He was terrified that if he let go he would be sucked into outerspace or something. He was excited and full of anticipation with this potential discovery but the concept of experiencing the unexplained was more than his young mind could handle. It was one thing to read about it, to study it and dissect it, but it was an entirely different beast to be in the middle of it. Brent and Alex in this way were blessed not having a purely analytical mind. Brent was the most impulsive of the three. He ran into a small clearing that was near the tree house.

"Come on you guys. I can feel it, it's right over here, WHOA!" With that exclamation his whole body lifted four feet off the ground. Travis held even tighter to a small tree, staring in disbelief. When he finally composed himself and had the presence of mind, he took out his digital camera and snapped some pictures. Alex stood frozen in place, too far from any tree to grab hold of it and afraid of befalling the same fate as Brent if she moved, waiting to see what was going to happen next.

Brent put his arms out straight, pretending to fly like superman. He achieved very little forward momentum. Then he started flailing his arms around, attempting to fly like a bird. It was then he was able to move forward and glide through the air. He would bump into a tree and push off with his legs to the center of the clearing.

"Oh wow, this is great, just too cool. Way too fun for words. Alex, come on. Push off of that tree and join me. No, push off hard and grab my hands and we'll see how high this will let us go."

Alex looked over at Travis, who was busily holding on to a tree for dear life with one arm and clicking off pictures with his right.

"Travis, you're going to join us? Right?" Alex was hopeful that Travis would let go and have a little fun.

"No, I don't think so Alex. Someone needs to document all of this."

"Oh Travis, we may never get a chance like this again!"

"I know, but if I don't take plenty of pictures and record what's happening, who will believe us. We're just kids for cryn'out loud."

"Have it your way," she said as she watched Brent do somersaults in the air, laughing the whole time, "but I'm going to push off...now."

She pushed as hard as she could and aimed straight for Brent. She grabbed hold of his hands and they spiraled upward an additional ten feet. That seemed to be all the force field would allow them to go. They squealed with joy as they tumbled and twirled. Travis snapped picture after picture, all the while trying to figure out how they were going to come down. Then out of the corner of his eye he detected movement. He turned his head to his left and saw a shadow that was not a shadow. It had a strange faint luminescence to it. Yet, it was translucent. He could only detect its presence when it moved. It was small in stature, about his height, maybe a little taller. The shadow was definitely a bi-ped and more humanoid than not. At least that was Travis's initial conclusion for he could not obtain any visual details of facial features, skin color, the number of digits on its hand, if it had hands. Travis turned his camera towards the shadow figure and zoomed in, for just a moment he thought he saw something come into focus. A bar of red light streaked down his body and flashed through the viewfinder. His body fell limp and he rose up in the air, about six to eight feet off the ground. Brent and Alex up to this point had been giggling and carrying on as though they had been on some new found amusement ride. Their carefree demeanor immediately changed when Travis's limp body drifted up. Brent tried to swim through the air towards him.

"Travis!" He yelled out. No forward movement came with the flailing of his arms as it had previously. "Ah Al, I think we are in big trouble. We've got to get out of here."

Brent no sooner spoke when the same red bar of light scanned his body and he too went limp. Alex's eyes widened with terror. She spotted movement near a large redwood tree. It appeared to be looking at some instrument it was holding in its hands. Then it aimed it at her.

***

A white van, which was following the convoy of trucks, had managed to get stuck in the mud, near the area where the threesome had first spotted the trucks coming down the dirt road to Crab Flats. The heavier vehicles had left deep ruts in the wet and soggy ground, which this particular vehicle landed in. The van was carrying very expensive electronic equipment. While the van was not geared for rough terrain, it was roomy enough to hold all the necessary electronic equipment. Inside the equipment was able to pick up minute changes in energy fluctuations, whether that was sound, light, or electrical. Ethan Bartholomew, referred to as Bart by his friends but 'Mad Bart' behind his back, climbed out of the van to assess the vehicle's demise. His driver had fruitlessly tried shifting from drive to reverse, rocking the vehicle back and forth, in an attempt to rock it out of the rut. Giving up, they both stood in front of the van. The van listed to one side, due to the front passenger wheel being buried in mud.

"Well, this is wonderful. We're on the verge of one of the greatest discoveries of a lifetime; no it's bigger than that. This is more important than man walking upright or the discovery of fire and here we are stuck in the mud. If any of this equipment is ruined, it'll be my head on the butcher block." Bart yelled in near hysteria.

"Bart, it's not like I did this on purpose." The driver snapped back at him.

"Well what are we going to do now, call triple A? I doubt very much they even service this area, not to mention that it would take them six hours to get here. By that time all those jar heads will have destroyed any evidence we came here to examine."

"We have a CB in the van. We can put out a distress call; I could get a fix on the military channel."

"Come on Tom, you know we are not even supposed to be here. Hacking the military channel will only get us prison time. I suppose we could hope a local is listening in, but with our apparent luck we would probably get a response from some truck driver in Arizona. You know how these signals bounce around in the mountains."

They both stood ankle deep in the mud, staring at the listing van. Bart kicked the tire, "Damn, so close."

"I'll go look for a piece of wood or something to use as leverage. I knew we should have loaded up one of the four wheel drives."

"There's no way all of the equipment would have fit."

"What good is the equipment if you can't use it?" Tom sniped.

"Just go find your wood. I'm going to see what kind of readings we are getting here."

Tom hiked up into the forest in search of something he could use and Bart slid back the van's side door. He flipped on the generator and then as soon as it hummed he plugged in his laptop and flipped a row of switches on the equipment inside. A program on his computer immediately started to decipher the information being fed to it. Bart plugged in a headset into the laptop and placed the padded ear set over his ears. He played with knobs, adjusting the sound level then he picked up a high-tech microphone and started panning the area. It was not long before he thought he had picked up an anomaly. He adjusted more knobs and entered some information into his computer.

"Well hello, what are you. Hey, where did you go?" He fiddled with some more knobs and switches. "There you are, let me just fine tune this a little bit more. Gotcha, now download to the GPS and we are on our way. You just hold still a little while longer, til 'Mad Bart' pays you a little visit."

Bart uploaded all the current data onto his laptop and packed his laptop with the microphone, headset, GPS and a Geiger counter, into a pack. He slung the pack over his left shoulder, placed the headset over his ears and flipped the hood of his jacket over his head. As he left the van, he turned off the generator and locked all the doors. Zipping up his jacket, to ward off the cold from a stiff breeze that had picked up, he spotted Tom with his arms full of bits of wood, pine tree branches and dragging a four inch round five foot long log. Tom was having a most difficult time keeping his balance as he came down the muddy slope. Bart got impatient at his progress and yelled out.

"Come on Tom…Ah geez." The sound pierced through his head and he quickly switched off the microphone. "We've got to go before I loose the signal."

"What signal and what about the van?" Tom shouted back.

"I picked up something quite interesting, just over there. I have a lock on it now, it blipped three times but now it's gone. I am also picking up a low gamma ray signature." Bart pointed in the direction the GPS had mapped out.

Tom stopped in front of the van and dropped the wood in front of the stuck tire.

"And again I ask, what about the van and all the equipment?"

"Well, you're welcome to say here with it, if you want. Otherwise, I am on my way. Come, stay, it makes no difference to me." Bart looked down at his GPS. "It's a good thing I uploaded the topo maps of this area before we came up. I think we can have a clear go at it if we start just up the road a bit."

"Your gut is telling you this is it, isn't it?"

"Oh yeah, Tom. This is the big one. The one that will put us on the front burner of the scientific community and make NASA envious."

"Or make us the laughing stock of the world with our faces splashed on every grocery store tabloid." Tom injected his take on the matter.

"Yeah and Galileo was accused of heresy. All great discoveries have their risks."

"Speaking of risks, you mentioned gamma rays. What's the reading?" Tom asked concerned for more than his ego.

"Not enough to worry about, at least not for twenty years or so."

"You're joking, right?"

"Come on let's go, we're wasting time."

Bart was known for his dry humor and Tom had a hard time with it. He was never quite sure when he was dead serious or just playing with him. Tom thought Bart liked it that way. He had been his apprentice at University of Redlands for two years. During those two years he came face to face with the truest definition of obsessive-compulsive behavior manifested in one person, that being Ethan Bartholomew. He thought Bart had watched one too many sci-fi movies and it had jaded a truly brilliant mind. Tom, on the other hand, did not possess Bart's passion. He drifted in and out from one interest to another, boring quickly and thus requiring a change of venue. In a way he envied Bart, his focus, his determination, and his passion. If it had not been for this sighting and the ensuing adventure, he had been prepared to inform Bart that at the semester's end he would be changing his major, again. Yet, here he was, once again tagging along while Bart was certain he was about to find his holy grail.

The road was now well behind them. Bart stopped for a moment to make sure they had not veered off course and to check his readings on the laptop. He signaled Tom to stop and be still. Holding up his microphone, he waved it slowly through the air. The sound of the wind whipped through the treetops. He edited it out. Tom cleared his throat. Bart rolled his eyes and edited it out. Shortly after he had honed in on a low frequency hum, he programmed his equipment to amplify it. This caused Bart to rip the headset off due to howling of a dog nearby.

Hugo was still at stay at the perimeter where the anti-gravity force field began. It spooked him and his sensitive hearing could detect a noise that told him to stay back. When the red bar of light flashed in the distance, a high-pitched sound was produced that human ears could not hear. Hugo started to nervously pace back and forth. He sensed danger and wanted desperately to be with Brent. Completely forgetting his command to stay and ignoring his own instinct to remain in his safety zone, Hugo at first ran along the perimeter deeper into the woods towards the general direction of the tree house. He stopped for a moment, sniffing the base of a tree, the tree where Travis had last hung onto for dear life. It was then his nose lifted into the air and he not only smelled Brent's scent but also saw his lifeless body floating in the air. This was when Hugo let out a howl that pierced Bart's ears. Tom stared at Bart with questioning eyes.

"Did that howl come from where I think it came from?" Tom asked.

"Yeah, I think so."

They both started running in the direction of the sound.

Movement, from the same area Travis had seen his shadow person, caught Hugo's eye. He growled and charged off in the direction of the movement. The same red bar of light hit Hugo in the eyes, he let out a sharp cry and his limp body floated up to join the others. Bart and Tom continued running through the woods, trying to avoid low branches and squeezing through thickets of brush. All the while, Bart held his GPS unit in front of him making sure they were maintaining a steady course to their final destination. Tom grabbed Bart's jacket arm. The pupils of his eyes almost completely erased the irises.

"Look." He whispered. "There in the clearing ahead. Are those bodies floating in the air?"

"Sweet Jesus, are they alive?" Bart asked aghast at what he was seeing.

"What can do that, Bart? Ah man, I think I just peed myself. What are we going to do? If what ever is out there can do that, what can we do?"

"Hold on, hold on. Let me think. Okay, I have recorded the sounds emanating from this area. I'll program sound frequencies on the opposite end of the spectrum, amplify it and what. I don't have speakers, I have a head set." Bart said thinking out loud.

"What about the speaker on the laptop?"

"It's not very powerful."

"Maybe if we get close enough, it will be powerful enough. You said it's very low, barely detectable. Maybe it won't take much to neutralize it."

"Maybe, hey do you have the binoculars?" Bart asked.

"No, I left them in the van. Why?"

"Those bodies look like kids and I think I see a dog in the midst of it all."

"Do you think that what ever it is out there knows we're here?" Tom's heart skipped a beat at the mere thought.

"God, I hope not. Keep your voice down and let me work on this."

Bart and Tom stayed crouched in the brush while Bart reprogrammed his computer. Then when he had finished he closed the lid.

"I told it to oscillate the sound frequency between the two I had detected. I sure hope the battery holds out."

"What way should we go in?"

"I think we will have better coverage if we stay to the left, away from the clearing."

"What if it has some kind of perimeter to detect our presence? I know I would. Maybe we should go back and try and locate the military. They would be better suited for this stuff than us."

"Tom, we're here now. We have a plan and it may be the only plan that just might save those kids' lives."

"And just might jeopardize ours."

"I told you from the get go, you didn't have to come along. You still don't, it's your decision."

Tom looked around, and discovered he had not paid much attention to the terrain as they hiked in.

"At this point, I don't think I could find my way back, even if I wanted to. Alright, let's do it."

Bart and Tom walked as carefully as they could, trying not to make any noise. They made sure they were under constant cover of the trees and the thickets. As they got closer they did not notice any change in the gravity as the kids had. It appeared it had been set to ensnare lighter animals not nearly two hundred pound men. When the floating bodies where in clear view, Bart opened his laptop and pushed a button and turned slowly in a circle. At one point the children's bodies lowered slowly about a foot closer to the ground.

"Bart, right there. Point that thing in that direction, it started to work."

Bart turned up the volume incrementally as he pointed the speaker in the direction that Tom indicated. To the human ear, no sound emanated form the laptop at all. Yet, it was having the desired effect. The children and Hugo descended. Just as with Travis, Bart noticed a movement out of the corner of his eye. At first he thought it was just a branch moving in the wind. Then a bar of red light streaked across his laptop. When he had made his calculations and programmed his computer, he anticipated that what ever had created this anomaly might try counter measures. So, he created a macro that would increase and vary in cycles. He was not quite sure if it was his program or if what ever was initiating the red bar of light had merely turned it off for its particular reasons. Nonetheless, the light was gone. He was thankful, very thankful. For he felt in that moment he was in the cross hairs of something he wanted no part. Then for just a moment he saw a shadow figure move behind a large redwood and for that moment, tiny little luminescent lights, ever so slightly lit up red to purple to blue then out. It was as if it had an emotional reaction and then it was gone.

The children laid lifeless on the ground. Hugo was the first to regain consciousness. He stood on all fours, shook from his head down to the tip of his tail, as a dog would when he shakes off water. Then he fell back down to the ground, looking like Bambi in the cartoon when he could not get his bearing on the ice. Hugo immediately got back up and shook off again. This time he stayed up with his alertness returning. Bart was apprehensive in approaching the kids with the dog now growling at him. Yet, he desperately wanted to move in and examine their condition. He took a step toward them and Hugo charged forward in his direction, barking and snapping at the air. Bart stepped back saying, in his calmest voice he could muster, "Good doggy, that's a good boy. I'm not going to hurt you or the kids. So, please don't hurt me. Okay?"

Dogs and Bart had never gotten along. His family never owned one but he had the privilege of getting bit by the neighbors German Shepard, twice. Therefore he was more than pleased when Hugo's attention was diverted elsewhere. That elsewhere happened to be right where Bart and Travis had seen the shadow figure. Hugo growled and then took off in a full out run at the redwood tree. Bart and Tom stared at the dog as he chased after the phantom through the woods. Once Hugo was a safe distance away, they approached the kids who were starting to awaken.

As Brent's eyes focused he realized that the person staring back at him was a complete stranger. In fact, initially he did not have a clue where he was or even who he was when he first awakened. Startled, Brent scooted back away from Bart, his eyes wide with fear.

"I'm not going to hurt you. We came to help you." Bart said reassuringly.

126

"Help me what? Why are Travis and Al just lying there? What did you do to them and who are you?" He asked in an accusatory tone.

"Honest, we didn't do anything. We were tracking energy signals from a UFO and…"

"UFO?" Brent said incredulously.

"A spaceship couldn't get here from …anywhere out there. It's just too far." Travis said as he regained consciousness. "Where are we and how did we get here?" He asked, trying to put the pieces together.

"You don't remember? Tom and I were tracking a signal and spotted all three of you…floating in the air…limp bodies just hanging in the air. Damn, it didn't look good for you guys."

"Floating in the air! I think I'd remember that!" Brent popped back.

"Well, remember it or not. I saw what I saw and I saw three lifeless bodies and a dog floating about twelve feet above the ground. Tom here saw it too." Bart said most emphatically.

The three of them stared at Tom, waiting for him to acknowledge or dispel what Bart had just said.

"I even got a few pictures of it. We were afraid that something awful had happened to you. I'd never seen anything like it in my life. I'm real glad you're all right. You are all right, aren't you?" Tom finally responded.

"Yes, I think so." Alex replied as she padded down her arms and legs to see if anything was hurt. "But I still don't understand how we got here or who you are."

"My name is Ethan Bartholomew. What was the last thing you do remember?" He asked.

"Sleeping in my bed." Alex responded.

"Me, too." Chirped Travis

"Yeah, dittos. You said you saw a dog? Where's Hugo? I never go anywhere without that blasted dog." Brent asked.

"He went that way. There was a shadowy figure just on the other side of the trees there…" Bart started to say but Travis continued the thought.

"There was a translucent image, with and iridescent glow, in the trees. I took pictures of it. I thought I was dreaming. Here, it's all right here on my camera."

Bart held the camera with the view screen towards him and pressed a green button. Images of the woods with Brent and Alex playing the anti-gravity game is what should have come up; instead each image was black as though there was no light at the time the picture was taken.

"Huh man, I know I got good pictures. This sucks." Travis remarked.

"Hmm, not only did this creature manage to wipe your memory, at least temporarily it appears it did the same to your camera." Bart shook his head in disappointment.

"I might be able to retrieve some of the images. I saw some gradation of light in a couple. I have a program that just might be able to restore the shots. Could I take the disk and see what I can do with it?" Tom asked.

"Yeah I guess but I'll need it back right away. It's my mom's camera and she'd have my head if I don't give it back with all its parts." Travis stressed.

"That's no problem. I can upload it on the computer in the van. Your mom will be none the wiser." Tom assured him.

"Speaking of moms, what time is it?" Alex asked.

"Just about one o'clock." Tom said as he looked at his watch.

"No, it's later than that. It is already starting to get dark. It's closer to four o'clock." Travis countered.

Tom looked around then at his watch again. "Son of a gun, it's stopped. Look the two little dots that blink for the seconds aren't blinking."

Bart always wore an old wind up watch his father had. It was the only memento his father had left behind. "Well it appears the boy is right. It is ten to four. We better head back to the van before it gets dark. I didn't notice any street lights on the road."

"Uhm, we're stuck in the mud remember or do we have an epidemic of memory loss?" Tom sniped.

"Ol'man Carpenter has a winch on his four by four. I'm sure he'd pull you out." Alex suggested.

"Yeah for a fee!" Brent added.

"Well I guess this ol'man Carpenter's lucky day because I'd be willing to pay just about any amount to get my van out of there tonight. I need to make sure all that equipment is safe and sound. He wouldn't also happen to have a room for rent?" Bart asked.

"He might, he has a spare room where his grandsons stay when they come up for the summer," Alex said with a worried look on her face and continued, "but if we don't get there soon he'll be eating dinner and he won't answer the door for anyone while he's eating."

"I still want to stop by the van, so I can up load young Travis's disk here."

"No, there's no time." Alex said with panic in her voice.

"Alex is right, there's no time. We have to be out of here before it gets dark." Travis exhibited the same panic.

"What's all the histrionics about?" Bart asked puzzled by their apparent need to get as far away from there as they could.

"It'll have even more of an advantage when it gets dark." Brent looked around trying to see any movement in the distance. "Then we won't even be able to see its shadow." He whistled then called for his dog. "Hugo, come here boy." He whistled again. "We've got to go now, dog or no dog. He'll find his way home. He always does." Brent made one last call for him then started out.

The kids led the way, taking their short cut through the woods back to their starting point at Holcomb Creek Road. They kept a quick pace, one that was difficult for Bart and Tom to maintain. For the most part, they quipped back and forth trying to come up with plausible excuses as to why they were late. Brent suggested that they lost track of time while playing games, which sounded good but that wouldn't explain the wet and dirty clothes. In between formulating alibis they would recant slivers of memories as they seeped back into the forefront of their minds. By the time they had reached Mr. Carpenter's house, the kids had remembered most of the recent events of the day and had agreed that the story was they had gone out looking for Hugo who had run off chasing a rabbit, cat, or raccoon. They were going to add they were afraid that Hugo would end up coyote food if they did not find him but thought better of it.

130

Brent arrived home before his parents had, to find Hugo sitting at the top of the stairs on the porch.

"Hugo, where have you been? Come here you bad dog. You gave me such a scare!"

Hugo stood but refused to come down the stairs. He did not even wag his tail or give him the usual "I'm so happy to see you smile," that Brent had come to know and love. This was the first unusual behavior Brent noticed in Hugo but it was far from the last.

Alex first took Bart and Tom to Mr. Carpenter's house then she went home. There she received a lecture form her mother, which she fully expected and was told she was grounded for the rest of the week.

Travis walked in the door to find his mother cooking dinner. Without turning around she told him to wash up and change his clothes because they were leaving directly after dinner to go the Community Center for a meeting. Apparently a representative from Twenty-nine Palms was to be there to give an official explanation, get damage reports, claims, and field questions regarding the previous day's incident.

The community center filled quickly; in fact it was over flowing. Many part-timers had come up to assess any damage done to their homes. Even though the local news had paid little attention to the story, with Green Valley Lake being such a small community, word traveled fast. Alex, Brent, and Travis joined up and sat off to one side, near the entrance. They were overwhelmed by the number of people there and how they did not know most of them, which was most unusual for they knew just about everyone. The chatter in the hall was almost deafening. It was nearly impossible to discern one conversation over another.

Mostly what they could pick out was regarding window damage to their homes but every once in a while some one would mention a UFO sighting and some one else would scoff at the notion. Just before the meeting was to begin Bart, Tom, and Mr. Carpenter made their way through the crowd and found a spot against the wall. This was on the opposite side of the room where the kids had found their spot, ready for a quick get away. Then just behind the kids a cameraman and a reporter set up at the back of the room, a few feet away from them. There was not an identifying logo on the camera or the reporter's microphone. Travis deduced it must have been an independent news source or tabloid but was glad some sort of news media was willing to cover this story.

Tony DiMaria, who was captain of the local neighborhood watch, called the meeting to order.

"Ladies and gentlemen, we need everyone to take a seat that is if you can find one. We don't have a microphone available on such sort notice so we will need the chatter kept down to a minimum so everyone can hear our guest. After our distinguished guest has made his statement, the floor will be opened up to a question and answer time and for those of you who have damage claims to submit, the forms will be made available at the end of the meeting. Members of the Green Valley Lake community please give a respectful welcome to Captain Michael Cooper from the Twenty-nine Palms Marine base."

There was a weak applause as Tony moved out of the way and the captain stood up. He started speaking without hesitation, his voice strong and commanding, which also matched his physical appearance.

"On Sunday the 27th of October, around 1530 hours, our radar picked up a fast moving object about 50 feet in diameter, traveling northeast to southwest. We had been informed that other stations as well as NASA had been tracking a meteorite and it was coming our way."

"A meteor, yeah right. That's a bunch of crock." Brent spat.

"At this time we had exercises in play which included Harrier jets practicing take off and landing procedures. Two overly zealous pilots took it upon themselves to track and follow this meteor to the crash site near an area known as Crab Flats campground. Due to their speed and low altitude, many of the residents here experienced window breakage to their homes. For this we apologize and intend to rectify the damage as quickly as possible. We currently have set up a containment area at the Crab Flats Campground, to determine if there is any possible radiation danger, and to perform any clean up if necessary. All unauthorized travel to this area is prohibited until further notice."

Mr. Carpenter jabbed Bart with his elbow, "Well, he finally got to the point. Now we know the real reason for this meeting."

"This is just a precautionary measure," the captain went on to say, "It does not mean that anyone here is in any danger, otherwise we would have started evacuation measures. Now if there are any questions, I will do my best to answer them." He finished.

Brent, Travis, and Alex decided they had had enough and left as three different people stood and tried to state their questions at the same time. They went outside to the beach area where there was a small playground. Alex and Travis sat on a swing and Brent leaned up against one of the swing set's supporting poles.

"You shouldn't have said that during the meeting." Alex chastised.

"Why not, it's the truth." Brent snapped.

"Yeah, but I was watching that cameraman and the reporter eyeing us after that. The last thing I want to do is talk to some reporter about all of this. I'd just as soon let everyone believe it was a meteor. For that matter, I wish I believed it was a meteor. It would make life a whole lot simpler." Travis lamented.

"I think we need to make a pact. We don't tell anyone anything. Deal?" Alex asked.

"Deal!" Brent and Travis both agreed.

They spit on their hands, then Brent stuck his hand out, palm up, then Travis placed his hand on top and Alex's hand on top of Travis's.

"Not even to those two guys, Bart and Tom. All we'll say to them is we don't remember. Right?" Travis added.

"Right!" Brent and Alex agreed.

That night, strong winds whipped through the area, bringing with it sheeting rain. The temperature dropped dramatically and the rain turned to hail. By morning's light, eighteen inches of snow had fallen and was showing no signs of stopping anytime soon. It was the heaviest October snowstorm anyone could remember for a long, long time. It snowed all the way down past the three thousand foot mark. The main road down the mountain was closed due to multiple mud and rockslides and a huge sinkhole had developed just past Running Springs. The Artic Circle was closed even to four-wheel drives with chains. The only other way down off the mountain was restricted to chains but that quickly changed with more mud and rockslides. Those now on the mountain

134

were staying on the mountain. Needless to say the schools were closed, and it would be days before any residential areas would see a snowplow.

Brent woke up to find Hugo sitting at his bedside staring at him. As soon as he stirred, Hugo whined.

"Go lie down, go back to bed. Bed, Hugo, bed." Brent rolled over and tried to catch a few more moments of sleep but Hugo whined again.

"Okay, okay, I'll let you go out."

The first thing Brent noticed was how cold it was in the house. He went over to the thermostat to turn up the heat but noticed the digital indicator was not visible. He looked around and noticed all the night-lights were out. Everyone was still asleep and now he knew why. The alarm clocks had not gone off because they had an outage. He figured as soon as he let the dog out he would wake his parents and let them know.

This was the second time he noticed odd behavior from Hugo. Hugo loved the snow. In the past, he had awakened him in the wee hours of the morning because he wanted to play in the snow. This time Hugo walked out onto the cold wet snow and stopped, turned around to look at him, lifting his paws and shaking them.

"Go on Hugo, go potty. Stop acting like a goof. You're not coming back in until you go. Go on, go." He closed the door. "Dang, it's cold…Dad, the electricity is out…we need to start a fire…quick."

Brent stood at the front window, staring out at the relentless fall of snow. His father walked into the living room, tying the belt to his robe. He opened the fireplace doors and threw in some wood and a couple of fire starters. As soon as it lit he stopped to take a look outside.

"Looks like we have our day cut out for us, so much for my morning meeting. If it keeps up like this, it'll be long into the afternoon before I'll be able to get the car out. We better change into warm clothes and get the boots on. There's a lot of snow to shovel. Did you check the phones?"

"Dead, dead, deadski."

"How about the cell?"

"Don't know. Bet we'll have over three feet before the day is through." Brent smiled.

"I just hope the electricity comes back on soon. We'll build up quite an appetite shoveling all that snow and right now our only option for cooking is that barbeque out there, covered in a foot of snow. First things first, we need to get a lot more wood up here. Where's Hugo?"

"Outside, taking a leak."

"He's got to be in seventh heaven."

"Not today, he's acting weird. I had to basically push him out the door and he just stood there, like he didn't know what to do, shaking his paws."

"That is weird. Well, you know what they say, animals take on the personalities of their owners," Brent's dad said as he ruffled his hair.

The electricity came on intermittently during the morning hours then finally stayed on later that afternoon. The snow plow never made it up Brent's street, but his dad was able to get the car down to a parking lot by the lake by that afternoon, in hopes he could at least make it down the hill the following morning. Parking was at a premium as many of the full-timers had the same idea. Some had already been bermed in by the snowplow. Brent and Hugo went along, Brent to help shovel out in the event the car got stuck in the snow and Hugo just because Hugo always went with Brent. As they parked the car, Brent spotted Travis and Alex walking across the street, heading for the little town market.

"Hey dad, is it alright if I walk back with Travis and Al?" He asked.

"I don't see why not. Here take some money and pick up... what was it your mother wanted...ah yes...a couple of cans of condensed milk. It's definitely a coffee day and we are almost out of creamer. Next time we are down the hill, we are going to have to stock up. It looks like it's going to be one of those winters," he said as he handed him a five-dollar bill.

"What about the change?"

"Get what you want. I'll see you back at the house. Don't forget the dog leash."

Brent snapped the lead onto Hugo's collar and called him.

"Come on boy."

Hugo balked at the prospect.

"Dog you are too much, first you didn't want to get in the car and now you don't want to get out. What is your problem?"

Hugo cranked his head to one side as if he was trying to understand the words he was saying, and then he jumped out of the car. They walked over to the store, where Brent tied him up on the front porch of the store, went inside, and met up with Travis and Alex.

"Hey guys, isn't this great?" Brent said.

"I suppose, but my arms are tired from shoveling snow. Hey did you hear that they closed down all the roads? They said it might be days before they can clean up this mess," Travis said as he rubbed his right arm.

"I heard they might have to do a helicopter drop with food supplies if they can't open the roads by the end of the week." Alex added.

"I heard they were already dispatching helicopters to the gi-reens stuck down in Crabflats. It appears they weren't prepared for such adverse weather." An adult voice said behind them.

"Hey Tom, where did you hear that?" Travis asked.

"Have a CB in the van, was listening in on the military channel. I know I'm not suppose to but I couldn't help my self."

"So you guys got stuck up here too."

"Yeah, ol'man Carpenter didn't have much in the cupboard so I came down for a few supplies."

"I can see that, looks like you're buying the store out. You walked down here?" Alex questioned.

"Yeah?"

"Well you have to walk back and that's a lot to carry." Alex retorted.

"No problem, I took one of Carpenter's grandkid's sleds. I'll just load it up and off I go. Hey, I see your dog came back." Tom said as he looked at the front door to see Hugo standing on his hind legs peering in the window of the door.

"Hugo, get down off of there." Brent yelled out.

"What's he doing?" Alex asked.

"I don't know. Come on let's pay and get out of here."

They paid for their items and quickly left. Brent grabbed Hugo's lead and yanked.

"Come on you goof ball, I'm taking you home. See ya latter Tom."

"Yeah latter." He said with a quizzical look on his face.

Outside, Travis stopped Brent.

"What was the big hurry?"

"I didn't want to talk in front of what's his name. I didn't want him asking a bunch of questions. I'm just glad it wasn't that other guy."

"Talk about what and why not in front of Tom?" Travis asked.

"Remember our pack, we're not suppose to talk about... you know...yesterday."

"What does that have to do with Hugo?" Alex interjected.

"Ever since the incident this dog has been acting weird. First off, when I came home to find him on the porch, I called him and he wouldn't come down the stairs, like he was afraid of the steps or something. Then this morning he acted like he had never seen snow. He wouldn't get in the car, then he wouldn't get out and then standing there looking in the window, like he was trying to hear what we were saying and I swear last night..." Brent stopped in mid sentence.

"What, what about last night?" Travis begged.

"I thought I was dreaming, but I had left my computer on, and I swear I saw him looking at the computer screen, like he was reading it. If that isn't weird enough I heard him go down stairs into the bathroom, like he always does to get a drink of water, but this time I heard the toilet flush."

"No way!" Alex exclaimed.

"I'm just telling you what I saw and heard." Brent said adamantly then he whispered, "I don't think that's Hugo anymore."

"What are you saying?" Travis asked, trying to think of the possibilities.

"I think..." Hugo tugged at his leash. "I think that what ever was out there is now Hugo." Hugo yanked hard and Brent lost his grip. The dog ran hard and fast away from the kids.

"See, I told you. He understood us and he's afraid someone will believe us. Come on let's go get him."

They ran as fast as they could. They started to catch up with him, only because it appeared he wasn't quite sure what direction to go. Then the dog ran up an unplowed street. Hugo had to struggle because the snow was up past his chest. The kids had it a bit easier since Hugo was acting like a small snowplow, making a path for them. The dog turned to see they were slightly gaining on him and ran behind a vacant house and stopped. Brent dropped his grocery bag, to make a last ditch effort to catch up with him. The dog looked up at the roof of the house, and the area where the electrical lines went into the house sparked. Brent backed off. He stood there with his mouth opened, his eyes wide. While he tried to catch his breath, the roof the house burst into flames.

"Geez Louise, can you believe that, he did that." Brent stared at the house while the fire sparked and the flames continued to rise. "We've got to get the fire department up here right away. Alex, your house is closer. Go call 911, I'm going to track Hugo," Brent said still in a trance.

"Do you think that's wise? If he can do that, not to mention what happened the other day at the tree house...I mean what else can he do?" Travis asked. "Ah, you do what you're going to do. We're going to get some help."

Alex and Travis ran to the house, only to find out that the fire department had already been called. Brent climbed up a small hill to see if he could catch a glimpse of 'Hugo'. There was no sign of his dog and his tracks disappeared right where he had last seen him. His eyes scanned the surrounding area looking for any movement, the fire cracked above him and he backed away from the house. Then to his left he thought he saw a movement out of the corner of his eye. A vague outline of his shadow creature appeared, a faint red glow ricocheted across what he thought was the creatures face, and then it disappeared. Brent thought better of pursuing the creature any further and went back down towards the street. Something inside him said he got his only warning.

Alex and Travis ran back down to find Brent just staring at the burning house.

"Where the heck are they? By the time they get here that house will be burned to the ground." Brent asked.

"Mom said it was called in, but they gave the wrong street and she's calling back to give them the right street. Look there they are, up there. Guess they didn't get the message," Alex said breathlessly as the fire trucks rolled up on the next street over.

"How come you stayed?" Travis asked.

"Got to thinking about what you said and it spooked me. It spooked me more than this fire. Wow, look at all the people coming out. Everyone is here before the fire department. Oh, oh, not a word guys. Here comes that Bart guy and Tom and a big, big plow with a fire truck right behind him. Don't think they can do much for the house but it's already spread to the telephone pole and that tree. I'm going across the street, get out of the way, and get away from the heat. Wow, just listen to it snap and crack." Alex said almost mesmerized by the fire.

The three of them found a safe spot across the street. Just as Bart and Tom started up a small hill towards them, Brent and Travis felt a hand on their shoulders. Brent turned around to see who it was.

"Hey Derek, what are you doing here?"

"Stuck on the mountain, like everyone else, watching a fire. Cool, huh?" Derek said.

"Not cool, you moron. That's somebody's house going up in flames." Travis snapped back.

"Derek? Derek who?" Alex looked right at him as she questioned.

Derek reached over and touched her shoulder. "Long time no see, Alex. How you been?"

"Oh, it's you, the jerk. Thought your parents sent you off to Switzerland or someplace."

"Annapolis, didn't like it. So, I'm back."

"You got thrown out of another school, huh?" Travis said with a condescending tone.

"Maybe."

"I'd give my eye teeth to go to one of those prep schools and you just don't care. What are you doing here anyway; don't you have some plush home in the valley?" Travis continued with the same tone.

"Dad and I came up to check on the cabin and ended up going to that meeting. Saw you guys there but you didn't stay for all the fireworks.

Dang, look at all the people coming out to see the fire. I didn't know there were so many people lived up here."

"My dad says they are just a bunch of 'yahoo's' come up to milk the system. Looking to get enough money to build a new deck or something, and most of these people are probably stuck here like you. Ah, garbage here comes…you know who." Alex retorted with the same tone she heard from her father.

Winded and obviously not prepared for the snow, Tom and Bart reach the kids.

"For a small town, you guys sure get more than your share of excitement." Tom remarked.

"Anyone know how this started?" Bart asked.

"No, unt ah. I haven't a clue." Brent quickly responded.

"Where's that dog of yours? Tom said he saw him when you were at the store. Said you said he had been really acting 'weird' since the other day." Bart asked.

"I think I said he was acting goofy. He always acts goofy. Sometimes I think he thinks he's a person and not a dog." Brent's voice was curt and just a bit defensive.

"Wow, you're about as warm and friendly as this weather. All I asked was, 'Where's your dog?" Maybe that incident out in the woods had more of an effect on you than you realize." Bart snapped back.

"What incident?" Derek asked.

"I'm sorry, it's just that fires make me really nervous, especially, after the Old Fire. Hugo is probably home, hiding. You know how fire spooks animals." Brent soothed his tone and gave what he thought was reasonable excuse.

"What incident?" Derek asked again.

"My program is in the last stages of deciphering one of those pictures. Once it has figured out one it only takes a couple of hours for the rest of them. You want to come over and take a look-see when they're done?" Tom asked.

Travis, Alex and Brent all looked at Tom with pleading eyes, as if to say, "Be quiet, don't talk about this stuff in front of Derek."

"Ah, come on guys. What incident? Are you talking about the meteor crashing? What? Give!" Derek insisted.

"We got lost in the woods trying to find where that meteor hit. Tom and Bart here, found us." Travis explained.

"And you took pictures of it, that's weird."

"Oh God, see what you started. Now he will never shut up. I'm out of here." Alex said with disgust.

"Yeah, let's go. The fire department has this under control. Besides I'm freezing." Travis added.

"Hold on, I dropped the grocery bag when I...saw the fire." Brent looked over where he thought he had last had the bag and saw part of the bag sticking out of the fire truck's tire tracks. "Oh great, I think it got run over." He added and went over to the bag and picked it up. Liquid ran out of the bag and he reached inside. One can was flattened and the other had a dent on one end but it still had its contents. "Well, one survived." He stuffed the surviving can in his coat. "See you later guys."

"Hey, come on guys. There's more to this story than you're letting on." Derek insisted.

All three kids turned and looked at Derek.

"Sorry Derek, you just don't need to know." Travis said with much delight.

"Ah, come on." Derek whined.

Brent and Alex both shrugged their shoulders and gestured as if to say, "I don't know what to tell you but I'm not saying another word."

Derek looked up suspiciously at Tom and Bart. Bart realized the kids did not want to talk about any of the past few days' activities. He did not want to jeopardize any co-operation and information he might be able to extract from them. So, he played along with their ruse.

"Hey don't look at me that way. You work it out with your friends. Come on Tom; let's go sit by ol'man Carpenters nice toasty fireplace." Bart said.

"Yeah, that sounds good. I think it will take me a week to defrost." Tom agreed.

While Bart and Tom were sitting in Mr. Carpenter's living room, sipping hot coffee and basking in the warmth of the fireplace, they talked about finding the kids in the woods, the evidence they collected, the fire, Hugo, and what they were going to do the next day. Tom took a sip of his coffee then looked up and stared at the window across the room. For just a moment he thought he saw movement outside the window. It was difficult to tell, due to the lack of light. The snowfall and the wind had kicked back up, making strange shadows from the swaying branches of the trees outside. His eyes searched the window for the movement to appear again. Then an image appeared in the window.

"Hey, isn't that that kid that showed up at the fire today?" Tom yelled out. "What the hell is he doing here, standing outside the window? Hey you, what are you doing here?"

Bart turned around to look out the window to see nothing.

"I think this place has you spooked Tom." Bart said disbelievingly.

"No really, I saw that kid. What is he doing out there?" Tom's voice was filled with panic.

"Tom, I'm supposed to be the paranoid one," Bart said as Tom raced to the front door.

"Hey you, kid. Keep your hands off that van. What do you think you're doing? Get out of here!" Tom yelled from the door.

The frigid wind whipped into the house, instantly cooling the room down. Bart ripped his jacket off the back of an overstuffed chair he had been sitting in and quickly put it on. He went to grab Tom and pull him out of the door way, but Tom had already bolted towards the van. The wind and snow pelted them as Tom slid back the door revealing the equipment inside.

"Tom, what the hell are you doing?"

"That kid, he was running his hand along the side of the van and the van started shaking, then he turned to me, smiled and then he was gone."

Bart stared long and hard at Tom, as though he were crazy.

"I swear to God, I'm telling you the truth. Come on, after what we saw the other day you're gonna give me that look?" Tom turned and flipped the switch to start the generator. Nothing happened. He fished out the van keys from his pant pocket, went around the front and jumped in the front seat, placed the keys in the ignition and turned them to start the van. Again, nothing happened. "I'll bet you ten bucks, all our data is gone too."

146

"You say it was that kid that was at the fire talking to Brent and Travis?" Bart asked.

"Yeah, but I have a feeling it wasn't a kid at all. I think what ever it was it is going about destroying all physical evidence that he, it, they were ever here."

A strong wind whipped through the trees. Bart tugged at the collar of his jacket, trying to give himself some protection from the cold. He placed his hand on Tom's arm.

"Come on Tom, let's go inside and get warmed up. There is nothing we can do about it tonight."

Tom sat for a moment just staring out the windshield that was covered with snow. Then he acquiesced and went inside to warm up. The electricity had gone out again and ol'man Carpenter lit a kerosene lamp. There was a long spell of silence. Then Bart finally spoke.

"Did you make back up copies?"

"Nope."

"Not even of the pictures off that kid's camera?"

"Nope, cut and paste. Didn't want them to have it, wanted it all for ourselves. So, we could have all the glory. Now we have nothing."

"How about the pictures on your camera?"

Tom started to laugh; it was a strange laugh, a haunting laugh. "It's in the van, I thought it would be safe there. Maybe the military had better luck than us."

"Maybe, but they are not known for sharing information." Bart said with a forlorn look on his face.

At early morning's light, military helicopters could be heard approaching the mountain. They made a beeline for the base camp set up at the Crab Flats campground. About a mile or so out they radioed in that they were having problems with the instrumentation and due to the rain were unable to obtain a visual. They were going to head up to Snow Valley and see if they could drop men, vehicles, and supplies at the parking lot by the slopes. By the time the ATV's arrived with the dry winter clothing the men were more than ready to don the jackets, gloves, and hats. Due to the change of plans with the drop off location, supplies would trickle in. Until the roads opened up, a sub-station would be set up at Snow Valley's parking lot. It was not an ideal supply line, but it would have to do for the time being.

The Log Cabin Café had electricity and was opened for business. The small restaurant was packed. Brent, Travis, and Alex wiggled their way through the sea of people to the counter. They each took a seat at the counter. The waitress was busy getting coffee for one of her tables. She turned, with her hands full, to see the kids.

"Hey, guys. I'll get your hot cocoa in a second. It's a mad house."

When she came back she tore open three packs of instant hot chocolate and dumped them into Styrofoam cups and added hot water then placed them on the counter. The kids were distracted watching a man who was talking to a sheriff.

"Here you go," She said expecting some kind of response. "Earth to Alex, Brent and Travis."

"Sorry Candy, who's that man talking to the sheriff? I thought I heard him say something about a missing kid?" Alex asked.

148

"Yeah, it's sad and scary. He and his son came up for the weekend to go fishing when all this hullabaloo occurred. Then the day of the Iris fire he just disappeared. They are trying to do a search and rescue, using us as their base, but with this weather…well just let me put it this way…nothing so far."

Alex had a pit in her stomach. She froze in fear but she knew she had to ask.

"What's the boy's name, and what does he look like?

"There's a poster on the other side of that pillar. What's the matter, you look like you saw a ghost."

"Nothing, thanks for the cocoa, Candy. Come on guys let's go."

"Al, we just got here. I'm barely warmed up." Brent whined.

She grabbed Travis by the arm, "Come on, now guys." Dragging Travis behind her, she stopped at the pillar and looked up at the poster. There staring back at them was a black and white picture with the name Derek Nolan underneath it. Alex turned to see the same horror in Brent and Travis's faces. "We've got to go."

"Where?" Brent asked

"Your house, it's our best chance for some privacy. Your parents tend to leave us alone and we need to talk." Alex said adamantly.

They ran into Brent's house, dropping coats, gloves, and hats in the entry way and quickly made it upstairs to Brent's room and shut the door behind them. Brent lay stomach side down on his bed. Travis sat at the foot of the bed, and Alex sat on the floor rug after she shoved a pair of dirty socks under the bed.

"Your room is a pigsty and it stinks." Alex grimaced.

"Well, you should feel privileged; you're the first girl besides my mom to ever enter my inner sanctum."

"Alex, how did you know the missing boy was Derek?" Travis asked with a most worried look on his face.

"I remembered you guys talking to him, and I didn't recognize him until he touched me, but I didn't remember that until Candy said a boy was missing. Then suddenly it all came flooding back, we don't know this Derek and we never have. It was him, it, the shadow creature from…has Hugo come back?"

"No, and it sucks. We've got to tell someone, maybe Tom and Bart could help," Brent lamented.

"I don't know. I heard Dad say that ol'man Carpenter has been telling anyone who would listen that he has two scientists staying at his house, and they are experts on UFO's. That he finally has someone who believes him about being abducted back in 1965. Dad says they are probably into 'junk science' and are on the payroll for some tabloid. So if we told Tom and Bart, who's gonna believe them?" Alex's body slumped in total discouragement.

"Yeah, ain't life grand? What do we have here, UFO's, little shadow people who levitate and zapped us unconscious with their ray beams, dogs that aren't dogs, missing kids who aren't human anymore, and the only people who may believe us are considered 'crack pots.' We're doomed. Can I wake up now? I'd like to have everything go back to the way it was when none of this was possible." Travis paused. "How about we just keep our mouths shut and stay right here until it's all over?"

"Only, if Brent cleans his room. From what I can see AND smell this is the place of origin of all things strange, unusual, and yucky." Alex said as her hand discovered a plate shoved under Brent's bed, still containing the remnants of a half eaten sandwich. "Gross, boys are so, gross."

Feeling safe from the outside world, they played video games. Alex particularly liked the one where they killed aliens and kept the world safe from enslavement.

Tom and Bart had spent the better part of the next day working on the van and the generator to no avail. Mr. Carpenter kept a CB radio in his 4X4 and had an old broadband unit in his house that he allowed his grandkids to play around on. So, Tom and Bart vigilantly sat and listened to the chatter.

Darkness had enveloped the Crab Flats Compound and the generators whined as they produced pockets of light in and around the tents. The snow had started back up shortly before sunset, and the wind howled through the camp taking the temperature down below twenty. A young soldier entered a tent filled with electronic surveillance equipment to relieve one of the soldiers of his duty. As he walked in, he pulled back the hood to his jacket and he could feel the hairs on his head and the back of his neck standing on end.

"Damn, there is a lot of static electricity in here." He said.

"Probably emanating from all the equipment," the other responded as he tapped the top of a piece of equipment. "Although, I am getting some strange readings. Look at this…it looks like we are getting a build up of a static charge."

"Can you tell where it's coming from?"

"I can't get a clear reading anywhere. Look it's jumping all over the place. We better call this in while we can."

The first soldier took his walkie-talkie off its holder and pressed the button to talk, but he got nothing but static. He walked outside the tent and tried again.

"24 Bravo, this is 18 Delta at the northern sector. We are getting erratic readings and a spike in static electricity. Do you read? Over." He released the button and listened.

All that spewed from the walkie-talkie was static. Then in the midst of the static he heard, "18 Delta, say again."

The young man was about to repeat his message when the other soldier ran out of the tent and pushed him aside.

"Get the hell out of here as fast as you can. There is a very serious overload and it's gonna blow."

A loud high pitch sound screeched from the walkie-talkie and the soldier dropped it to the ground. He ran as fast as he could to catch up with the other soldier. As he did the ground beneath him began to shake and blue and white arcs whipped out of the tent and snapped upward and outward. Falling to the ground, he looked up into the sky, just above the tent. The arcs of electricity looked as though they were touching something like little fingers feeling their way across a large metal object, but it was difficult to see what through the snow whipping through the air. Then the ground shook even more violently and a lightening bolt came from above and hit the tent. For just a moment he thought he saw a very large odd-looking spacecraft hovering above the tent. As quickly as the image appeared it was gone and all that was left was the tent and all of its equipment on fire. It was not long before other soldiers arrived with fire extinguishers but there was nothing left to save.

The only good thing about snow, lots of snow, was that Travis, Brent, and Alex would have another day off of school. They all would have normally been okay with the snow days but after what had happened in the past couple of days, all of them looked forward to life getting back to normal.

Alex tossed and turned in her bed. She had a very uneasy feeling most of the evening. Bennie was asleep at the foot of her bed and as she rolled over, yet again, the dog growled.

"Sorry Bennie." She said as she looked down at him. His eyes glowed back at her, as a dog's eye does when you shine a flashlight at them. This spooked her, especially after what had happened to Hugo, and she grabbed her robe and ran into her parent's room.

"Dad, can I crawl in with you? I had a bad dream."

"Sure pumpkin, climb aboard." Her dad said half asleep. "Just like old times."

Alex snuggled in between her parents only to find Callie had already beaten her in, with her entourage of stuffed animals. She squeezed in between Callie and her Dad, pulled up the blankets and stared at the ceiling.

Travis was sitting at his computer. He had logged on to different chat rooms trying to find out if anyone had any more information regarding the sighting. He came to the conclusion that they were mostly Aunt Sandy types who could barely carry on a conversation that included a complete sentence. He was about to shut down and crawl back into bed when he noticed there was a build up of static electricity in his room. The hair on his arms stood on end. He could even feel the hair on his head rising. Afraid to touch his computer he pushed his chair away, but when he went to get up he inadvertently touched the table where the monitor and keyboard were and an electrical current sparked. The snap of current went all the way up his arm, then the monitor went dark, and he could no longer here the hum of the CPU. Travis scrambled under the covers of his bed and then tied himself to the bed. Earlier that night he had an uneasy feeling that something was going to happen, and he was afraid they, it, what ever it was, was coming back for him. He wanted to make sure that he was not taken easily.

Brent's bedroom window faced the back of the house. He liked it because on the nights when there was a full moon it shined in his window, illuminating the whole room. When he would look out the window the moon lit up the landscape behind his house. It would create eerie shadows but he always thought it was kind of cool, the stuff of the creep shows he loved to watch. There was no full moon tonight, yet as he looked out his windows he thought he could see those same eerie shadows, only this time it gave him the creeps. He missed Hugo something fierce. There next to his bed rested Hugo's empty bed with his blankie neatly folded on it. He searched the darkness in hopes of seeing him run up to the back door as he had so many times before. There was no dog in sight. Just as he was about to crawl back into bed, Brent thought he saw something move in the distance. The wind changed directions and the snow with it a faint image of what looked like a small person stood in the snow below. The shadow sparkled with neon blue light then disappeared into the night. Brent crawled under his covers, remembering what Travis had said earlier and had taken several belts and linked them together and tied himself to his bed.

Tom was all but asleep, with his head resting on the table where the broadband radio was kept, when the radio cracked with excited voices. It was difficult to discern what was being said because it sounded as if everyone was trying to talk at once. The best he could make out was something was happening down at Crab Flats, something big. He went in and woke Bart up who in turn rousted Mr. Carpenter out of bed.

"Fred, what ever it is, it's happening now. All signs point to Crab Flats."

"Well, we better get a move on before all the fireworks are over. One doesn't usually get a second chance at these things."

Tom and Bart, with Mr. Carpenter behind the wheel, squeezed into the front seat of his 4X4, and as fast as the roads allowed, drove towards Crab Flats road. The plows had not been through since that evening's snow started coming down, and even with four-wheel drive the going was tough. As they drove past the little café, Fred noted how odd it was to see the lights on there so late. He was just about to turn down Crab Flats road when his headlights shown on a person standing in the middle of the road. He hit the brakes stopping only a few inches from a boy standing naked in the road. Next to him sat a dog. They both had an empty look in their eyes and did not budge an inch when the car nearly hit them.

"Lord, have mercy on my soul. Where did he come from?" Fred spat in utter amazement.

"That's that kid that was lost in the storm." Bart shot back.

"Hell, that's that kid that messed with our van." Tom shivered.

"Who ever he is, he's a kid standing naked in the middle of road almost getting plowed over. Grab that coat in the back seat. We've got to get him somewhere warm, quick!"

Tom reached around and grabbed an old parka, jumped out and threw it around the boy. Fred was hesitant about reaching for the dog but soon realized the dog was in the same daze as the boy. Bart sat frozen in his spot, realizing they were probably going to miss what ever it was out there in the darkness. His eyes searched the blackness past the light of the headlights to no avail. So close, he thought to himself, so close. Tom and Fred brought the boy and the dog into the SUV and took them to the café. It was a very long night with a bittersweet reunion.

The morning's light showed no more signs of snow. The sun shone brightly as the town woke to a new day. The boy was transported to the mountain hospital. He showed no physical signs of harm, but he was unresponsive. The Doctor declared that Derek was in a pervasive catatonic state. Hugo remained dazed and lethargic for a few days then one day woke up to his old self. It still took a few more days before the roads opened up down the mountain. The military was the first to pack up and leave. As soon as the part-timers who had also been trapped on the mountain left, the small community resumed its peaceful and uneventful demeanor. Bart and Tom had the van towed back to the university; it appeared that everything electrical had been fried. The high school erred on the side of caution and waited four more days before reopening. It was not until the kids went back to school did they realize that they had missed Halloween. The threesome agreed that with all that had happened, it was no big loss.

That spring, Brent, Travis, and Alex were walking down Lakeside Drive with Hugo leading the way. It was the weekend before Memorial Day and the lake had just been stocked. They knew Memorial Day weekend it would be too crowded to fish so this was their best chance to fish in their favorite spot. The canoe was ready for use and locked up at a tree just a few feet from shore. Alex had her fly pole and a pair of waders. She knew the boys would row out as far away from her as possible, but that was just fine with her. Her dad said he would be down as soon as he was done with his 'honey do' list. The warmth of the sun fell on her face, and she smiled at the thought. It would be just like old times. Brent and Travis were being their usual silly old selves, making bets on who would catch the most fish. Brent had a dollar on Alex, two to one that she would blank. Alex did not care, not one little bit. She knew in her heart there would come a day she would out perform them all.

They were about two hundred yards from their final destination when Hugo took off and ran up onto the front deck of a house that had recently sold. There sitting in a chair with a blanket over his lap, sat a boy about their age, a frail and solitary image of a boy just staring out at nothing. Hugo licked his hand and nudged him with his nose, trying to get a response. A man walked through the opened door and watched with a cautioned curiosity. Brent followed Hugo onto the deck. Travis and Alex followed close behind Brent.

"I'm sorry Mister. I don't know what got into him," Brent said as he tried to get Hugo to leave. "Come on boy." Brent pulled on his collar. Then he looked at the face of the boy and realized it was Derek. "Oh, he's the...you're his...?"

"I'm Mr. Nolan and yes this is Derek my son and this must be the dog they found with him that night."

"Yes sir, it appears they have a special bond."

"It appears so; look at his hands. They're twitching, and his eyes are moving back and forth. This is the first response of any kind since that night. I knew coming back here would help. It's been a long haul for us, first with his mother passing then this."

Alex looked long and hard at the boy, first trying to recognize him. Then she realized something.

"Travis, he looks like you do when you are heavy into typing something on your computer. Look at him, he looks like he's typing and reading but really fast."

"Do you have a computer in the house?" Travis asked.

"Just my laptop. Why?"

"I have an idea."

Mr. Nolan picked the boy up and carried him into the house and sat him down at a table. Travis opened up a notepad document and placed the boy's hands on the keyboard. As soon as Derek's fingers touched the keyboard the page filled up with ones and zeros.

"It looks like garbley gook." Brent remarked.

"No, it's code. I haven't a clue what it means but its computer code alright." Travis deduced.

"Well, I don't care what it is. It's the first time since…" A tear ran down his face. "I'm just glad you three…" he looked over at the dog lying next to Derek… "you four came by today."

"We're really sorry about your boy, sir," Alex said, not sure what else to say and feeling most awkward. "How long do you think he'll sit there like that?" She added amazed at how fast he was typing.

"Probably awhile, I think they put a whole lot of info in that brain of his and it will take a while for him to get it out." Travis blurted out.

Both Alex and Brent stared at him.

"What!" Travis snapped.

"We agreed. We made a pact." Alex barked.

"He has a right to know. It's his kid for crying out loud, it directly affects him." Travis barked right back, which took Alex off guard.

"They who, what are you kids talking about?" Mr. Nolan asked. "Are you talking about the rumors and innuendos about UFO's and alien creatures that supposedly landed here last October?"

"Not rumors." Brent said.

"Not innuendos." Travis added.

"Not supposedly, unfortunately." Alex grimaced.

"Not that I believe any of this stuff but I think you need to tell me what happened, at least what you think happened." Mr. Nolan motioned for the kids to sit on the couch.

"Alex, you're better at this than us. We'll jump in if you forget something," Travis pleaded.

Alex did her best to tell the full story but as quickly as she could. She was concerned that her Dad would panic if she was not where she said she would be. It took about an hour when all was said and done. Mr. Nolan's head was spinning but when he looked over at Derek he was not quite sure if there was not more truth than fiction to their tall tale. As they started to leave Brent called for Hugo but he would not budge.

"I'll come by later to get Hugo. I guess he needs to be here."

"Oh, Mr. Nolan? If and when Derek completes what ever it is he is typing, you might want to contact Ethan Bartholomew at Redlands University. I think he would be most interested in this." Travis added.

"I think I will do just that young man. This has been a most interesting and promising day."

It was almost two weeks before Derek stopped typing, and Hugo came home. Mr. Nolan was most concerned about Derek's health during this time. He had to force-feed him soups and Jell-O, and by the end of it Derek had lost a few more pounds, weight that he could not afford to lose in the first place. Once Derek had stopped typing he rested his head down on his arms and fell into a deep sleep. Mr. Nolan picked up his frail body and tucked him in bed. He was prepared to take him into the local hospital the next day if he did not show any signs of improvement. That next morning held a very pleasant surprise for him. Derek awoke weak and disoriented. He called out to his father who ran into his room.

"Dad, where are we? I can hardly move, what happened to me? Oh man, I am so hungry. I feel like I haven't eaten in a week." He looked up at his dad with pleading eyes, so full of confusion.

"One thing at a time, son. First let's get your strength back and fix you a nice breakfast."

Mr. Nolan called Ethan Bartholomew and told him what happened and Ethan arrived at his doorstep two hours later.

"I'll return the laptop as soon as I upload it to another computer."

"That may take awhile. The hard drive is full and it's an eighty gig hard drive."

"Eighty gig's, all in code you say."

"Yep, pretty much all in code."

"I think I have my work cut out for me for a very, very, very long time."

Due to his youth, Derek recovered in no time. He did not remember a thing from the day that he was reported lost and after awhile he was fine with it. Travis, Brent, and Alex adopted him into their little group and they never broached the subject again. As far as they were concerned the incident at Green Valley Lake was just rumors, speculation, and innuendos, something best left for the science fiction writers.

THE END

Biography

I was born in Jamestown, New York and I am currently living in Southern California with my husband Doug and our dog and two cats. In 1992, I started portrait drawings after having the misfortune of working in a bank that was held up twice in forty-five days. The second robbery was a violent takeover. My adventure in drawing was my way to keep in touch with those things in this world that make life worthwhile, those things that illustrate the glory of God. I began my pursuit of writing shortly after my father, Donald V. Gustafson, died. Here I found a way to express my emotions through various characters in stories. Grieving is a process, which is different for each individual who must labor through it. Whether I was faced with the grief of the loss of my security in the workplace, facing the terror of the possibility of the loss of my own life, or the actual loss of a loved one, I have chosen to take what I consider the most positive and constructive course toward my own healing, this being through painting and writing. I hope you have enjoyed the end product of my journey.

www.ingramcontent.com/pod-product-compliance
Lightning Source LLC
Chambersburg PA
CBHW051829170626
46807CB00003B/1090